The Vow of
Parvati

The Vow of Parvati

ADITI BANERJEE

BLOOMSBURY

NEW DELHI • LONDON • OXFORD • NEW YORK • SYDNEY

BLOOMSBURY INDIA
Bloomsbury Publishing India Pvt. Ltd
Second Floor, LSC Building No. 4, DDA Complex, Pocket C – 6 & 7,
Vasant Kunj, New Delhi, 110070

BLOOMSBURY, BLOOMSBURY INDIA and the Diana logo
are trademarks of Bloomsbury Publishing Plc

First published in India 2022
This edition published 2022

ISBN: PB: 978-93-54355-05-9; eBook: 978-93-54355-11-0
2 4 6 8 10 9 7 5 3 1

Typeset in Manipal Technologies Limited
Printed and bound in India by Replika Press Pvt. Ltd.

To find out more about our authors and books visit www.bloomsbury.com and sign
up for our newsletters

PART I

SATI

CHAPTER 1

One day, as Sati wandered through the sylvan mountains of Mount Meru, stroking the white flowers adorning the blue-green trees, she glanced up and saw a purple constellation hovering high in the sky. *How lovely this shade of violet would look in my hair,* she thought. Immediately, she leapt up and landed on that distant moon. She was a devi, after all. What could she want that would not appear before her in the blink of an eye?

This moon truly was violet, with swirls of marbled purple like the most luxurious of cushions. She nestled against the pocked surface with a contented sigh, letting her black tresses float into the inky, cold air. The endless night did not frighten her. Being at a different end of the universe from the only home she had known did not frighten her. Nothing had frightened her yet.

She stretched her legs, her crimson toenails and bell-hung anklets gleaming even brighter than the moon. She crooked her fingers at the neighbouring stars and they obeyed, shrinking into the size of crystals as they fell softly into a pile on her pink silken veil. She sifted through them delicately, balancing them on her soft palms, admiring their shape and shine. She whispered her benediction upon each and sprinkled them around her neck. They beaded into a multistranded necklace, cool and glittering against her skin. How precious these stars were, dearer to her than the celestial gems back home that were exquisite and rare, wrought by divine hands, embedded with incantations and the powers of the devas.

She caressed the stars that cuddled into the folds of her neck, naming them. She wished she could rest there for thousands of years. Then she realised with a gasp that she was late for the assembly of the devas. She sat up, the stars fluttering around her neck anxiously. A few twirls of her fingers rearranged them into prettier constellations floating into the darkness. Perhaps no one would notice her handiwork in this remote corner of the universe, but nothing satisfied Sati like beauty and harmony, and she could not resist making every place she visited more pleasing to the eye.

'Brahma may be the Creator,' she whispered to them, 'but males just don't have an eye for this sort of thing.'

They nodded with twinkles and giggles that sounded like the rippling of a brook. She smiled at them, brushed the stardust off her pink dress and vaulted into space.

♋

Sati descended into the skies of Mount Meru, hopped onto a cloud and whispered into its wispy ears to hurry to the assembly hall. It was time for all the gods and goddesses, the devas and devis, to congregate in the assembly hall to receive the sacrificial fire offerings from the mortals through the daily yajna. Sati's father, Daksha Prajapati, presided over the rites like a strict taskmaster, and he would be furious if his daughter was late.

Daksha's pride and joy was being appointed as the officiating *purohit* for the yajnas for the next several thousand years. He took this seriously. A little too seriously, if you asked Sati or her mother, Prasuti. But Daksha never asked his wife or daughter for their opinions.

Sati jumped off the cloud onto the golden steps of the assembly hall. A thousand stairs led up to the pavilion where the immortals and the sages, the wisest of men and women, congregated. She glided up the steps, her slippered feet barely touching the smooth metal.

Sati's eyes scanned the assembly hall as she walked into the seated throngs of devas and devis. Daksha, her father, was in the centre, presiding over a large fire pit. The musky scent of *samagri*, the offerings of wood, leaves and medicinal herbs picked by the humans and offered into the sacrificial fire, emanated from the *yajnashala*.

Her rightful place in the assembly hall was by her mother, behind her father. In ordinary circumstances, she could have flown or apparated to her seat. But using such powers during the sombre sacrifice was against protocol. During yajnas, the devas strove to be humble and grateful for the offerings. The focus was on sending back blessings and benediction. The yajna was foundational to maintaining the rhythm of *rtam*, the cosmic order and balance of the universe, the consecrated interaction between the divine and the mortals. The devas treated it with due gravitas. Sati's fingers fluttered against her pink satin sari, as she wondered how she could sneak to her seat without breaking the rules.

Her father's voice rang out coldly, 'Chitragupta! Who is missing from the ceremony?'

Chitragupta, the keeper of records, said, 'Missing? The assembly is full, sir.'

Daksha harrumphed. 'I've been counting footsteps and I know that at least two pairs are missing. It is your duty to take roll call. Now report who is not here.'

Chitragupta sighed and yielded, reluctant because he was fond of Sati. 'Rudra is missing and...'

At that moment, Sati's eyes found Narayana's across the hall. He was sitting on the highest dais, the one reserved for the most exalted devas. She widened her eyes in supplication, and with the hint of a smile, he lifted his right hand a few inches. The radiance of the Sudarshana Chakra, the golden serrated discus that was poised above his index finger, blinded everyone in the vicinity. They instinctively moved away, shielding their eyes from its light.

Even Sati wanted to look away. The chakra discomfited her. She did not know why. After all, the blue-hued Narayana was her brother-in-law and the Preserver of the worlds, the most compassionate of the devas. He had always been kind to her. But the chakra sent cold waves of energy to her heart. She sometimes imagined the sensation of the chakra tearing her body into pieces.

You are being silly, she chided herself as she proceeded to her mother's side, landing in a rustle of pink satin. She threw a grateful glance to Narayana. He winked at her.

'And who?' demanded her father sternly.

'Sati,' replied Chitragupta with a gulp.

'Sati!' exclaimed her father, whirling around to face her.

Narayana said, 'Well, as you can see, she is right here. It is only Rudra who is missing.'

It was deft of Narayana to turn her father's attention back to Rudra, whom Daksha despised. It distracted him from Sati's tardiness.

'Rudra! Well, that rascal never shows up. He is surely out with the night demons, surrounded by ghastly ghouls and goblins, getting intoxicated. He would only contaminate the sacrifice.'

Sati winced. Daksha was brash to speak so disrespectfully of the greatest deva, who had beheaded Brahma, Daksha's father. Daksha was nothing in front of Rudra. He had got away with this impudence so far partly due to his prerogative as the officiating *purohit* of the devas and partly because many secretly agreed with him, wishing that the fiercely powerful Rudra would just be a little more civilised. *It was all well and good for the asuras to behave like that, but Rudra should show some more class.* They whispered this way while sipping soma from their gem-encrusted goblets, as their eyes darted about in fear of being overheard by Rudra and then, possibly, beheaded. They need not have worried. Rudra was oblivious to them all.

Sati had never met Rudra, nor did she want to. He sounded downright terrifying and rude. She loved only that which was beautiful. She closed her eyes, dreaming again of starlight and a purple moon.

The yajna took hours. It was the only time of the day when all the devas assembled together. Mount Meru was the abode for all the devas, where they congregated. The prominent devas and devis had their own *lokas*, each realm with its own city and palaces, weather systems and internal law and order.

Other than fighting the chronic wars with the asuras and saving the worlds from one disaster or another, sacrifice was what brought the devas together. It was the sacred covenant that bound the entire cosmos, maintained the seasons, tides of the oceans and the settlement of the tectonic plates. During the yajna, the devas received the oblations that the mortals had offered into the fire and prayers written on leaves floated down sacred rivers. They listened to the whispered mantras uttered in their honour, prayers whispered on bended knee. These sounds and the scents of the herbs, wood, and food purified by the sacred flames wafted into the bodies of the devas and sustained them. It was more nourishing and pleasing to them than food, which they took only once in a while as indulgence. And, in return, the devas breathed out benediction, boons and blessings that were carried back by Agni Deva into the smoke of the fires tended by men, drifting into their beings and altering their lives and destinies in subtle and auspicious ways.

It was Agni Deva, the very embodiment of the sacred fire, who served as the medium and mouth of the devas, who accepted the offerings and conveyed them to the devas. Agni Deva dwelled in both mortal and immortal realms, and on behalf of the devas, he received the offerings. And again, on behalf of the devas, he offered the fruits of the yajnas back to the mortals. It was for this that he was the first to be invoked in the sacred Vedas; it was for this that fire was the one element of Earth that could never be contaminated. Water and air could, but never fire. It purified all.

Sati emerged from the assembly hall, calm and content. She slipped away through the woods winding down the mountainside of Mount Meru, eager to escape her father in case he was still cross with her. She had recently moved away from her parents' home and been granted permission to reside with her two sisters. They were not genealogical sisters, but the three were the triumvirate of the foremost devis and thought of themselves as sister devis—Saraswati, Lakshmi and Sati.

Their home was close to the assembly hall so that the elders could keep an eye on them. Crowds awaited hours each day just to catch a glimpse of them as they returned from the assembly hall. Sati's eyes scanned the crowd of supplicants gathered along the ten-thousand-step-long stairway carved of rose-coloured ice, which led to the entrance of their home. As an added security feature, the ice could turn into a flame with the briefest of mantras. That was Sati's role, one she rather relished.

Gold lanterns flickered along the edges of the stairs. Aged rishis with flowing white beards gently murmuring hymns from the Vedas lined the stairs on one side, and an assortment of animals and divine beasts on the other. There were the usual—elephants, horses in every colour of the rainbow, giant eagles and even some squirrels. They were all gazing hopefully at the golden doors. Sati suppressed a smile.

This was all Lakshmi's doing. She loved to feed wild animals, and now they came like clockwork to feed from her hand. Sati preferred quieter things that did not move or talk, like the stars, the sun and the vast, endless skies. She liked that which reminded her of the eternal, unchanging substratum of reality. She liked that which had no beginning or end, no limit at all.

Wanting to avoid the crowd, Sati sneaked in through a side entrance, vaulting from the evening sky puffed with dark clouds into the kitchen window. Her dramatic appearance sent the *gandharva* cooks scurrying. They hurriedly prostrated themselves in front of her. She smiled sheepishly and gestured to them to rise. The devis did not need to eat, but Lakshmi liked to sample different cuisines and Saraswati liked to hear the *gandharvas* tell their stories the way only the bards could. Sati liked to close her eyes and imagine the exotic settings they described. They inhaled only a few spoonfuls of food, giving away the sanctified remains as prasad.

By the time Sati entered their private sitting area, Lakshmi and Saraswati were waiting for her. Saraswati, resplendent in white, eternally ethereal, looked at Sati with glowing brown eyes.

'Late again, dear sister? You narrowly escaped being in trouble with your father!'

Lakshmi looked up from the couch where she was lounging, her chin resting on her daintily stacked hands, a coy glance flickering through her long lashes. Lakshmi was so stunningly beautiful that sometimes Sati had to look away.

Lakshmi said, in a mellifluous voice tinged with pride, 'By the grace of my husband.' She was newly-wed enough to blush shyly at the mere mention of Narayana.

Sati nodded. 'Yes, my brother-in-law is very kind, indeed.' As she plopped down on the floor between her two sisters, Sati added, 'I suppose I should be grateful to the delinquent Rudra, too, for absorbing the brunt of my father's anger, leaving very little for me.'

Lakshmi laughed, but Saraswati stiffened at the mention of Rudra. They rarely spoke of him in front of her. Rudra had decapitated one of the five heads of Brahma, the Creator. Brahma had grievously insulted Rudra, and Rudra, being quick to anger, had plucked one of Brahma's heads with his fingernails. Saraswati had never married, but she was close to Brahma. She, the goddess of wisdom, always buried in books and spells and music and the arts, could never be far apart from the Creator. Sati left her to her secrets and past.

Sati thought it best to change the topic, 'Speaking of your husband, Lakshmi, why is it that you are still living here with us spinsters? Shouldn't you be in Vaikuntha?'

The highest of the celestial abodes, Vaikuntha, was the realm of Narayana. Lakshmi shook out the vermilion skirts of her sari, setting the bells of her golden waist belt tinkling in a pleasing melody. She sniffed.

'Hmmph. He is about to avatar off to some world, out to save the mortals once again. I would rather be here than in Vaikuntha alone right now.'

Sati's ears perked up. 'Is he going to Earth?'

'No, Earth has its charms. This is a very unpleasant planet. The land is covered with constantly erupting volcanoes. You cannot imagine how disgusting it smells, like ten million rotting eggs. And the creatures are quite rude. They don't care whether you try to help them or show them kindness. They just try to claw you and eat you.'

Saraswati tsk-tsked sympathetically. 'Poor brother-in-law in that horrid world, all by himself without you for comfort.'

Lakshmi bristled. 'Not without me. I am right there in his heart.'

It was not just figurative. Narayana literally bore the mark of Lakshmi on his chest.

Now Lakshmi wanted to change the topic, 'Speaking of marriage, Sati, I dare say it is your turn to get married. Our other sister is quite hopeless, but it is just about time for you to marry.'

Sati shook her head and rolled her eyes.

Lakshmi let loose a peal of laughter. 'My dear baby sister, who in the heavens will we find to be your husband? You are the gentlest, most beautiful, most graceful devi to ever set foot in Swarga. Who could possibly be good enough for you?' She thought for a few moments. 'Thirty-three million devas and I can't think of one suitable groom. We will have to create another Narayana just for you.'

Sati groaned. 'I love my brother-in-law, but I do not want to marry another like him.'

Lakshmi slanted her almond eyes at Sati slyly. 'Then whom would you like to marry?'

Sati shrugged. 'I do not know.' And it was the truth. She had never thought about marriage or romance. Her head was always in the stars, dreaming about worlds in which no one existed but her.

Saraswati chimed in, 'You better think fast, Sati, or all the devas will be taken, and you will be stuck with Rudra!'

They all laughed heartily at that.

CHAPTER 2

Sati gazed at the red orb pulsing above her palm as she walked the marigold-strewn path to the house of her guru, Brhaspati. He was teaching her and the other students world-building. Their assignment was to create and bring back a sample world for inspection.

In reality, it was Narayana who breathed all the worlds into existence. And Brahma managed the logistics of the climate, ecosystem, rules and forces by which animals and other mortals would live and die there. But it was the belief in Devaloka that all the principal devas and devis—the ones fit to be called Iswara or Iswari—should be skilled in the functions of creation, maintenance and dissolution. Even though these abilities were inborn for this cohort, they still learned from the guru to exemplify for others the importance of education and reverence for the teacher.

Sati shielded the orb with her other hand. Garuda, Narayana's giant eagle *vahana*, who was circling overhead, had an insatiable curiosity. If she were not careful, he would swoop down and peck at the delicate red world she had built, damaging it permanently. She had poured all her heart into it.

Sati entered Brhaspati's hut. It was in this simple, thatched dwelling—meticulously swept clean of the flower petal offerings left by Brhaspati's countless disciples and admirers—that Sati had first met Brhaspati's wife, Tara, the devi of the stars.

Sati usually preferred to roam alone, but Tara was one of the few whose company she enjoyed. Since Tara was her guru's wife, Sati prostrated before her and was gently raised into Tara's embrace. Tara was lithe and radiant. The whites of her eyes gleamed like starlight and her skin, with a faint blue sheen to it, was dusky like evening.

Rumour had it that her marriage to Brhaspati was uneasy. Sati herself sensed it. Tara was quiet and restless in his presence. As revered a scholar as he was, Brhaspati was obsessive about his wife, fearful of losing her. Once, it was said, she had had an affair with Chandra, the ruler of the moon. They had chased each other across the skies, giggling and flirting during the long pursuit, relishing the 'hunt'. Finally, he had captured her. Loath to leave, she had begged Brhaspati to let her, the queen of constellations, to remain with Chandra, the king of constellations—like among like. But Brhaspati was too besotted with her to let her go and dragged her back to their home in Swarga after waging a few celestial wars with Chandra in the process.

However, Tara was already pregnant with the son of Chandra. The poor child was born only half-formed. He lived in perpetual confusion about who his father was—the guru or the moon. He lived a life of limbo, the lord of the planet Mercury, mercurial in nature.

'Just goes to show,' Saraswati had said with a smirk when they had gossiped about this in the past, 'learning is not the same thing as wisdom. He is learned enough to be the guru to the devas but not wise enough to know how to manage his marriage or when to hold on and when to let go. He is a priest, a scholar, firmly tied to this Earth. But she is of the galaxies, of stardust and comets, meant to live among the skies.'

It had sobered Sati to realise that even devas couldn't avoid misery. Sati squeezed Tara's hands, balancing the orb above her head as they sat down to drink hibiscus tea. She reminded herself to take Tara out for a walk among the stars soon to keep her entertained. Sati inhaled the delicate aroma of the pink tea and let out a contented sigh.

'What lovely tea, Tara Devi. How do you make it so special?'

Tara leaned in with a conspiratorial wink. 'I add a sprinkling of starlight.'

They giggled as Brhaspati walked in, fresh from a bath in the portion of the Ganga River that flowed through Mount Meru. His appearance was in stark contrast to that of his wife—thick-bellied with dishevelled white beard and hair. Sati immediately prostrated herself in front of him, and Tara lowered her head in a mark of respect. The usually bubbly Tara immediately became demure in his presence.

It was unfair, really, Sati thought to herself. Tara belonged to the class of ancient deities who were of the elements, free and spirited by nature. It was her right to go where she wanted and be with whom she pleased. All these notions of modesty and chastity were new and in vogue among the current generation. But it had not always been like this, and the newfangled notions should not be imposed on the elders, believed Sati.

Sati followed Brhaspati behind the hut. It opened onto a lovely expanse of grass bordering the river, convenient for his bathing and rites. Woven branches provided shade above a wooden desk where he sat to read palm leaf manuscripts. There was a fire pit for his yajna, a circle of cushions where he taught and a cluster of trees where he meditated with students. He may have been an unsatisfactory husband, but Sati could find no flaw in Brhaspati as a teacher. He did not instruct others on anything he had not tried and practised himself, prizing the direct, individual experience of *aparoksha jnanam* over the indirect, intellectual knowledge of *paroksha jnanam*.

Brhaspati sat with a sigh, his joints creaking. 'Come, child, let me see what you have done.'

Sati knelt before him respectfully. She proffered her hand, bearing aloft the crimson world she had created. He smiled at her, charmed by her eagerness. He wished all his students were as dedicated.

He softened his voice. 'Shall we enter?'

'Yes, please,' breathed Sati. Brhaspati's instruction had been to create small handheld worlds. Planet-sized worlds could cause cosmological chaos. It was not worth disturbing the work of Brahma, the Creator, Narayana, the Preserver, and Rudra, the Dissolver, over such trifling assignments. Instead, when each student came before Brhaspati, he would expand the world to inspect it. The universe could manage one rogue planet under Brhaspati's careful supervision.

Brhaspati gently tapped the red orb with his finger. Immediately, it ballooned up and out. And in the next second, Sati and Brhaspati were inside the world she had created. The sky was the colour of a rose petal and the ground was soft as velvet, pastel pink sand swirled with orange. The strumming of a veena could be heard all over. Fragrant floral gardens proliferated around them. They wandered for some hours, traversing gently undulating meadows filled with shimmering golden grains that could be picked and eaten raw. There were no mountains or volcanoes, no difficult terrain; there were murmuring lakes but no oceans with wild tides.

Brhaspati tested the ground with his feet. It was spongy and soft. 'What is the foundation of this planet, Sati?'

She frowned. 'The foundation?'

'What is at the core, that which holds your planet together?'

Sati shrugged. 'I had not thought about that. I just filled it with enough soil and dirt so that all the crops and plants could grow, so that everything would live comfortably.'

Brhaspati shook his head with a smile and continued his inspection.

Sati hurried after him. 'Revered guru, just see the creatures of this world. They will enchant you.' She fluttered her arms, whistling for them to come. They emerged from their hiding spots behind the trees and ran towards her. There were baby elephants as small and cuddly as puppies, gigantic swans with wings that unfurled into the colours of the rainbow, soaring horses that floated through the skies, dolphins that you could ride leaping through lakes, across forests and up the hills. Brhaspati nodded indulgently and waited as Sati demonstrated all their talents and beauty.

After some time, he turned away. 'Come, child, it is time to go.'

Reluctant as she was to leave this world of hers, she was eager to hear her teacher's comments. She followed him obediently. He tapped the skies with his finger, safely reducing the planet to an orb once more, and then with another tap, dissolved it into a thin red trickle that he wiped off his palm.

Sati asked worriedly, 'Did I not do well?'

Brhaspati gestured to her to take a seat as he sat cross-legged at the low wooden table. 'The world you created is very pretty, Sati. But it cannot last. It would collapse onto itself.'

Sati frowned. 'Why? What did I forget?'

'Sati, tell me, when is a flower the prettiest?'

She said immediately, 'When it first blooms in the spring after the winter snow melts. Or in the crack of a mountainside, surrounded only by dirt, where the air is inhospitable, yet it still grows.'

'Yes. Why is it so?'

She had to think about it. Beauty was instinctive, intuitive to her, not something she ever analysed.

'I suppose it is because of the contrast. Something delicate, like a flower, against the hardness of a mountain. One can only know warmth if she has experienced coldness.'

He crinkled his eyebrows fondly. 'Yes. When building a world, when building a life—even one's own personality—there has to be balance. There have to be opposing forces that come together in harmony.' His eyebrows set into a grave expression. 'I know you must think I am a poor husband for Tara, that she deserves someone more romantic and passionate. And perhaps there is truth in that. But it is also true that someone as ethereal and elusive as my wife needs someone to ground her. And someone as nose-deep in the texts as I am needs someone to pull me away from the ground. We have not yet found that happy balance, but I hope one day we will,' he shared rather self-deprecatingly.

Sati's cheeks pinkened to be privy to such an intimate confession. She kept her eyes trained on the ground demurely.

Brhaspati knelt down next to her and said in a gruff voice, 'Ah, child, why do you think I'm telling you all this? Just for a world-building lesson? One of the thousands of exercises you've gone through in your studies? No. Sati, look at me. This is important.'

She slowly looked up into her teacher's eyes.

'Sati, everything about you is refined, gentle, beautiful, sweet.'

Her voice soured. 'You make it sound like a bad thing.'

He chuckled. 'They are all very good qualities. The question is whether, as a devi, you want to remain restricted to those qualities or go beyond them to something higher. Do you know, Sati, there are two types of devas and devis? The first type is known for one or two special qualities, worshipped for them and is able to bestow blessings only tied to that quality—it could be beauty, intelligence or great martial strength. The other, the far, far rarer variety, may display an affinity for a few qualities but has transcended them, therefore, they are capable of bestowing all blessings, summoning all powers without limitation. They are the ones who can rightfully be called Iswara or Iswari, who are bound by nothing and who are supreme.'

This was not something Sati had considered before. It opened up new vistas in her mind, new ways of perceiving

herself and the devas around her. 'How can you tell one
type from another?'

'Ah, that is a good question. It is not easy. It can be
very subtle. It can be difficult even for other devas to
judge. It is one of the secrets of the universe. But this
much I will say, child. Having been a guru to the devas
for aeons, I have seen thirty-three million of them come
and go, and you, my dear, are special. You can be so much
more than what you are today. You can be one of the
supreme ones, unlimited, the greatest of the great.'

Sati asked hopefully, 'And then the world I created
would be able to survive?'

He laughed. 'Oh, so much more than that, Sati. With
that transcendence, with that balance and power, you
sustain not just one world but all the worlds... Existence
itself.'

Sati was sceptical. Sometimes, he did exaggerate. She
prostrated. 'Please instruct me, gurudev. I will try my best.'

Brhaspati patted her head affectionately. 'Just think
about balance, Sati. Start with that.'

♋

After leaving her teacher's hut, Sati went on a long walk.
She was determined to work on balance immediately. She
went to one of her favourite spots, the No-Name Tree. It
was one of the very few sites in Mount Meru that did not
have its own name and official history. The tree was of no
known variety. It produced tiny orange fruits that were
bitter, sour, tart and sweet, all at once. It was said that once
an apsara and *gandharva* had fallen in love and met here.
Their appointments kept them in remote corners of the

universe, and it was only under this tree that they were able to meet in interludes of hundreds of years. From the tears of their parting after each bittersweet reunion, it was said, this once barren tree started bearing fruit. Even though the couple had long since disappeared, each evaporating into the elements, the tree remained standing as a testament to their rare love and kept bearing fruit.

It was quiet here. The denizens of Mount Meru preferred places with a happier history, hallowed by the footsteps of the great sages, not a hapless couple with a doomed future. That suited Sati fine since she enjoyed her privacy. She leapt up to the topmost branches, spreading her green veil to blanket her from the thorns. This was an incredibly tall tree. She seemed to be resting a yojana or two up from the ground, at least. She nestled her head against the fragrant deep green leaves, tossing a few orange berries in her mouth, before closing her eyes.

She began her meditation with the flower-strewn path winding across the mountainside. The warm colours of orange, yellow, pink and red spread across the red clay tamped smooth by millions of years of footfall. The colours dissipated into the light fragrance that rode on the breeze, wafting its way up to her nostrils and caressing her hair. This made her smile. Up she floated through the azure sky, not a cloud in sight, waving a lazy hand at the passing sun and soaring eagles, until she drifted into the galaxies beyond. She floated into the world she had created, determined to fix it.

Sati did not know that she was not the only one meditating on the No-Name Tree that day. She had been too enraptured as she leapt up into its branches to notice there was another meditating at the base of the tree.

Sati reminded herself that she was supposed to be practising balance, to introduce different forces into her world that would contrast and complement what she had created. What was the opposite of colour and warmth, the opposite of fragrance and beauty? She intended to conjure a vision of falling snow, cool, white and yet still pretty, something to dampen yet not kill the flowers. Before the first white drops could fall, a sudden gust of ice tore through the world. The roar of a thousand shrieking winds split her ears. Sheets of grey water fell from the suddenly dark skies and froze into layers of ice that fissured the ground into crevasses. Her feet slipped from beneath her, and she tumbled down into one of the dark cracks breaking apart her world.

Sati cried out and found herself back again in the No-Name Tree. She had lost her perch and was plummeting down to the ground. Normally, she would have been able to right herself in time to break her fall, but she was still in shock. Suddenly, the speed of her descent slowed until she became as light as a feather and came to a standstill a few inches above the grass, lying on her back as if on a blanket suspended in the air.

With a gasp, she turned to see what kind of protective net had caught her. There was nothing but empty space between her and the grass. Then, from the corner of her eye, she saw a blue-green hand resting on a tiger skin, the thumb pointed upwards. As her breath settled, the thumb folded itself into the palm of that hand and she landed softly on the grass.

Sati hastily got up and brushed the leaves and orange flowers off herself. Her hair had come undone and she nervously tried to pull it back together. She did not want to appear dishevelled in front of the stranger.

She need not have worried. That stranger was thoroughly impervious to everything around him. His eyes were closed, body immobile, breath imperceptible. Had Sati not seen that subtle movement of his thumb, she would have thought him a corpse. Her mouth fell open at the sight of him. She had never seen anything like him in all the worlds. He sat cross-legged, a scrap of tiger skin covering his waist and upper thigh. A small rivulet of water trickled down the knotted tawny manes of his hair, which was almost as long as her own, falling wild and untamed across the expanse of his bare back. In its topknot shone a small, glowing white moon. He wore no jewels, but his body appeared to be covered by a fine grey-white powder that smelled fragrant even from a distance.

Sati leaned in closer. She may as well get her fill now, she thought to herself, since he appeared to be sleeping. She could look at him for hours.

A red little goblin spat at her feet and hissed, 'Get away! You cannot disturb his meditation!'

Sati snapped back, 'Disturb his meditation? He is the one who broke mine!' She could not tell how but she was certain that it was he who had intruded into the world of her reverie and ruined it.

The red goblin, as high as her knee, hopped over until his webbed toes were less than an inch from Sati's slippered feet. There was a distinctly unpleasant odour to him. He was pot-bellied and ugly, his red face wrinkled like the hide of an elephant, with hairy ears that were disproportionate to his pinched face.

She regarded him calmly.

He folded his paws and said matter-of-factly, 'Devi, please keep your voice down. Trust me, you do not want to rouse him from his meditation. He can get angry...very angry. It is for your sake that I am urging you to walk away.'

Sati was not the type to be easily irritated, but something about that meditating blue-grey figure provoked her. 'Well, if he can't be awoken by a woman falling out of the tree under which he sits, I don't think my standing here is going to bother him.'

The goblin sighed deeply.

'Oh, don't worry. I'm leaving.' Sati hurriedly put her hair and dress to rights. She was on her way to see her father. She was a mess, hair hopelessly knotted, smudges of orange berries dotting her dress, which also had small tears from where it had snagged on branches. Her father absolutely would not approve of this whole affair.

Before leaving, she turned around, ignoring the exasperated hiss of the goblin, knelt on the grass and prostrated herself to the one who meditated at the base of the No-Name Tree. She had been so jittery earlier that she could not even process who she was looking at, overwhelmed as she was by his presence. But now that she thought about it, he could only be Rudra.

She whispered, 'I have never met you before, but of course, I know who you are. How can I not? How could anyone in Devaloka not? You are Rudra. You are Mahadeva. I offer you my reverence, Mahadeva.' She hesitated, but then the words tumbled out anyway. 'I suppose I should thank you for saving me from falling, even though I would not have fallen if you had not interrupted my reverie with such a terrifying vision. As Mahadeva, you should have perhaps realised I was there and taken better care not to disturb me.' She nodded in satisfaction at the prayer she had crafted, offered another prostration and then rose and walked away.

Had she dared to look back, she would have seen the curving of those stern lips into a slight smile.

♋

Sati played Chaturanga, a strategy-based board game, with her father by the firelight. This was her favourite time with him. He would get so engrossed in the game that he would forget to lecture her. He took pride when she won, and even when she was on the verge of defeat, he would give her hints on how to come back and bare his king. There was nothing he loved more than indulging her happiness—within constraints.

That evening, Sati was distracted. She could not stop thinking about Rudra, and made mistake after mistake, causing her father to grunt in dissatisfaction. He tapped the eight-by-eight Ashtapada board to draw her attention. Vishwakarma, the architect of the devas, had carved the board and the pieces from a million-year-old tree in Amaravati, the abode of Indra, king of the devas, which Dhanvantari, the healer and health-giver among the devas, himself tended as its leaves and bark were of great medicinal value. The pieces were smooth and heavy in Sati's hands, their eyes glowing with inset rubies.

Her fingers played with the messy braid she had managed to tie her hair into. She tried to introduce the topic casually, as one would discuss the weather. It was even more boring to talk about the weather in Mount Meru than in the mortal world, because the weather ran like clockwork there. There was only pleasant, slightly cool and slightly warm, with a light drizzle or snowfall on occasion to break the monotony.

'Pitashree, I think Rudra is back in Mount Meru.' She tried and failed to stop the blush creeping up her cheeks at the mention of his name.

Daksha snorted. 'Of course, he is. How could anyone not notice? The ruffians he associates with create such ruckus. It's disrupting all of Mount Meru.'

Sati thought of that red goblin. She had heard that Rudra mingled only with *ganas*. The *ganas* were impossible to define. They were an assortment of creatures who accompanied Rudra in the cremation grounds and in Mount Kailash, his abode. Some were frightful in appearance, deformed and dwarfish. They paid no heed to societal conventions, roaming around naked and drunk, intoxicated with the love of Rudra. They were Rudra's dearest companions.

'Why does he associate with *ganas*, Pitashree?'

Daksha grunted. 'Don't ask me to create logic where there is none. Anyway, he always comes back this time of year in preparation for the Night of Rudra.'

The Night of Rudra was that one night a year when all the creatures of the universe fasted and stayed awake in the worship of Rudra. Even the devas observed this *vrata*. This was the first year Sati was old enough to join the devas in the assembly hall, where Rudra would preside in the centre, accepting all of their offerings.

They played silently for a few minutes, when Daksha spoke up, 'Sati, be careful of him. Keep your distance. He is very hot-headed. I do not want you to be in any danger.'

She trained her eyes on the chessboard. She thought of that flick of the thumb that had kept her from crashing into the ground, how that small movement had protected her.

'I do not think he will do anything bad to me, Pitashree.'

He grunted again, his fingers trembling slightly around the gaja or the elephant piece in his hand. Sati reached out to clasp his hand.

'Why do you worry about me so, Pitashree?'

His eyes met hers, troubled and stormy. 'You are so sweet, Sati, so innocent. I am a hard man, but the world is a hard place. It is my duty to protect you from all the hardships and cares of the world.'

'But we are in Mount Meru,' she said with a smile. 'We are safe here.'

His voice rasped. 'That you are innocent enough to think that—Sati, that is exactly why I must protect you. I can bear anything but cannot bear for you to be hurt in any way. You are the best of all my daughters, and I will see that you get only the best of everything in life— the best home, the best education, the best food, the best clothing and, one day, the best husband. I will protect you from all harm. That is my purpose in this life.'

Sati's eyes clouded with tears. She remembered Brhaspati's lesson from earlier in the day, which already seemed so long ago. That what seemed best on the surface was often deceptive, that the world and she needed balance. And she thought again of how, in one movement of his thumb, Rudra had balanced her in midair. It was a moment she could not forget.

♋

It was to her sisters that Sati spilled the full story when they were in their beds at night. They each had their own room but used their supernatural hearing to whisper through the walls.

Lakshmi teased, 'How romantic, really!'

'Hmmph!' retorted Sati. 'Hardly romantic! He was not even awake.'

Lakshmi rolled over to face Sati on the other side of the wall. She whispered conspiratorially, 'That makes it even more romantic…that he could sense you even when unconscious.'

Saraswati pointed out dryly, 'You know, Sati is actually a devi and perfectly capable of protecting herself. She could have suspended her own fall. Whatever movement of the thumb you saw or thought you saw could perfectly well be a random coincidence. You both are reading too much into nothing.'

That deflated the chatter for a few minutes.

Lakshmi giggled. 'Well, the only way to know for certain is for you to ask him the next time you see him, Sati.'

'Never!' exclaimed Sati. 'Who knows if I will ever see him again. And even if I do, oh, I could never bring myself to talk to him like that. He is so very—'

'Frightening?'

'No, not frightening, exactly.'

'Terrible? Grotesque?'

'No, no, no. He is just overpowering.'

Lakshmi's voice grew teasing again. 'Overpoweringly attractive?'

Sati blushed, her fingers outlining his invisible form in the moonlight streaming in through the window. She replied shyly, 'That's not what I meant. But… he does have a very nice fragrance, there's this fine white powder that covers his body… it's—'

'Ash,' said Saraswati acerbically. 'It is ash, dear sister. Ash from corpses in the cremation grounds that he smears across his body every day. That's what that powder is.'

Sati's throat turned dry.

Saraswati continued, 'And while you were enraptured by his "fragrance" and the movements of his thumb, you may have failed to notice the long black serpent coiled around his neck.'

Sati's hand fell to her blankets. She began to feel ashamed of how she had been romanticising him to her sisters.

Saraswati's voice softened. 'I am not trying to be cruel, Sati. But whatever you feel for this Rudra, you must see him with your eyes open. You are the one who was repelled by his presence, by that icy vision he conjured around you. His very aura disturbed you. If you want to be attracted to him, you must accept that other part of him, too. Do not be selective in your perception of him.'

Sati nodded against her pillow. 'As always, sister, your words are sobering and wise.'

'He is Mahadeva. You cannot hold him so easily in your mind. He is not easily captured, even by thought,' said Saraswati.

Of course, that made the rebellious part of Sati want to capture him even more.

CHAPTER 3

A few days later, Sati was taking her usual evening walk when the sound of the veena tickled her ear. The single floating high note was so sublime and achingly melancholic that it made her pause mid-stride. She loved music and had never heard a veena sound that way. Curiosity got the better of her, and she began following the sound.

She walked and walked, past the dimly glowing coloured lanterns of the populated part of Mount Meru into dark lanes that were not illuminated by lanterns or the brilliant gems Mayasura cleverly placed in the walking paths to provide light from below. After some time, the path itself became indiscernible. It was only due to the faint moonlight filtering through the canopy of tree branches above that Sati could see where she was walking. There were no footprints to follow.

The note itself had faded away, but after what seemed like an hour, another note sounded. This one was low and so deep that it made her very bones tremble. She could hear a distant beating drum, rhythmic and slow. It made her heart beat faster and she picked up her pace, even though she was a bit anxious to be in a wilderness she had never before explored.

Yet, the music beckoned her on, further into the night. It unfurled slowly, one long note at a time, but it was bewitching all the same. Some primal instinct within her drew her inexorably forward, placing one foot in front of the other, over and over again, until she found herself at the edge of the mountain. At the end of the lane was a fenced-off area. It seemed a ramshackle abandoned plot—boulders strewn across the lawn, a haphazard proliferation of strange trees and plants, some that looked to be from far-away galaxies—but the thatched hut at the corner had a lamp burning in front of one of the windows.

Sati leaned against the fence to try to peer into the hut. But she was too late. The music had drawn to an end as soon as she approached the fence and now there was only silence.

She sighed wistfully. She was about to turn away and head back home when she saw a small white flower blossoming on an overgrown tree just beyond the fence. The flower was so exquisite that it made Sati lose her breath. She clambered on top of the fence to get a better look, bending the bough towards her. She had seen millions of flowers in her lifetime but never one like this. Its folds were tightly wound into concentric diamonds wrapped into a circle, its inner petals alternating gold and silver. The scent was subtle yet lingering, milky and musky. She bent her head and inhaled deeply the fragrance from the soft yet sturdy petals.

An outraged squawk caused her to almost fall off her perch on the fence.

'You! You came back to steal from our lord's garden.'

Sati's mouth fell agape as she looked down to see that same red goblin, his paws indignantly held akimbo. The clamour drew out Rudra and Chitrasena, the chief of the *gandharvas*, from the dimly lit hut.

Chitrasena exclaimed, 'Sati, daughter of Daksha Prajapati! I never would have expected to see you here.'

Sati did her best to offer her prostrations to both Rudra and Chitrasena, although it was rather awkward to do so from her half-crouched position on the fence. *I must look so ridiculous*, she thought in embarrassment.

She was too modest to realise how radiant she looked at that moment, her face like a moonbeam, framed by the dark green foliage shimmering in the silver moonlight.

Rudra approached, shooing away the red goblin until he stood directly beneath her, looking at the small white flower clutched tightly in her hand.

Sati blurted out, 'I am not here to steal the flower, I promise! I had just come to hear the music, and then I saw it and it looked so beautiful, I just wanted to see it better.'

Rudra said nothing, deftly disentangling the branch from her fingers. She had grown so flustered that the flower had bruised slightly. With a few flicks of his finger, Rudra restored the flower to its original bloom. He pinched it off the branch and held it in front of Sati.

She winced. 'Oh, you did not need to do that. It would have been better to let it live.' As much as Sati loved flowers, she never plucked them. She thought it cruel to kill a flower just so she could enjoy its beauty. She only collected and adorned herself with flowers that had already fallen on the ground.

'But I am the god of death,' Rudra replied smoothly. His voice was like the ocean, unfathomable and still, ancient and bottomless. It sent a thrill across Sati's spine. 'And it is for me to make sure that whatever lives, dies well. Far better for this flower to die early, in the hands of one who loves it, than to die forgotten and alone in this remote corner of the universe some weeks or months from now.' He placed the flower in her palm without touching her.

'I shall take the very best care of it,' Sati promised, gently caressing the petals. She was uncharacteristically shy, unable to meet his eyes.

Chitrasena cleared his throat. 'Come, Sati, I was just about to leave. I will walk you back. You should not travel this far unescorted. Let me just collect my instruments.'

There was an awkward silence as Chitrasena left Rudra and Sati alone. Well, Rudra did not appear awkward as he stood there, unflappable as a statue, neither acknowledging nor moving away from Sati. It was as if she had stopped existing. But she certainly felt awkward.

She groped for any topic of conversation and seized upon music. Chitrasena was the best of the *gandharvas*, and the *gandharvas* were known for being master musicians and storytellers.

Sati said cheerfully, 'I think it is wonderful that you are learning music.'

Rudra finally moved. He turned his head towards her, arching a tawny eyebrow. Sati continued eagerly, now inspired, 'And, of course, Chitrasena is the very best to learn from, as the *gandharvas* are so skilled in music.'

Rudra gave a dismissive sniff.

Sati thought he was scoffing at the idea of learning music. 'No, no, it is really a very good skill to learn. Especially for you.'

Rudra's eyebrow inched up higher.

Sati rushed to explain, 'I mean, you are so very wild and isolated. Music is very... beautiful. I think it will make you more sensitive. My teacher has just been instructing me about the importance of balance and being multidimensional...' Her voice trailed off as she thought about how ridiculous she must sound.

Luckily, Chitrasena appeared and they were able to take their leave. As Chitrasena opened his mouth to utter his farewell, Rudra simply turned around and walked away.

♋

Sati and Chitrasena began walking back to her home. Chitrasena was whistling the tune of a ballad of forlorn lovers. *Gandharvas* were romantic like that. Sati was gazing in adoration at the flower, which shimmered brightly in the darkness around them. It perplexed her that someone like Rudra was capable of cultivating something so delicate.

Sati waited until Chitrasena was between songs before she asked, 'How long have you been teaching music to Rudra?'

Chitrasena broke stride and almost stumbled off the edge of Mount Meru. Sati caught his sleeve and pulled him back. He was a tall and imposing male figure, handsome with long midnight-black hair and sharp features, a silver filigree crown on top of his head.

He gawked at her, eyes wide with disbelief. 'Me? Teach Rudra? Music?'

Sati's face contorted in confusion. 'Isn't that what you were doing there? After all, *gandharvas* are experts in music.'

Chitrasena laughed, a charming sound that boomed like a roaring waterfall. 'And from whom do you think *gandharvas* learnt music, Devi?'

Now it was Sati's turn to stop and look at him.

Chitrasena shook his head and sighed. 'Sati, how can you not know that Rudra is also Nataraja, the creator of all music and dance?'

Sati flushed beet-red. Now she remembered the strange look Rudra gave her when she had told him she was happy he was learning music from the *gandharva*.

'I did not know,' Sati said woefully.

Chitrasena arched a brow. 'How could you not know, as a devi, having lived here so long?'

Sati bit her lip. 'My father does not like to speak of Rudra.' She remembered how sublime that music was, how it reached the deepest recesses of her inner being and cast her under a spell. 'I just cannot imagine how someone so cold could produce something so beautiful.' She was thinking of both the music and the flower.

Chitrasena observed her for some moments. 'There is a lot about Rudra you have yet to learn, Devi.'

♋

The next few days Sati devoted wholeheartedly to the flower. She experimented by placing it in bowls of water, keeping it in soil, muttering mantras over it; however, it bloomed best when tucked into her hair. Its shine and fragrance delighted her. Every sniff suffused her with a rush of euphoria. At night, she placed it next to her pillow so it would not be crushed. When she bathed, she used a few drops of water to cleanse the petals as well.

She thought it would die within hours or days, but the flower flourished under her touch. There was magic to it that she did not yet understand.

Everyone who saw her admired the flower, some rather covetously. One day, Sati, Lakshmi and Saraswati visited Amaravati, the abode of Indra, king among the devas. Shachi, Indra's wife, had invited them for a picnic. It would have been rude to refuse.

They wandered slowly through Indra's palace. The diamond-encrusted pillars and gold furniture were so gaudily bright that Sati's eyes hurt. The scent of roses wafted through the air. A constant low refrain of a song played on a veena echoed through the eight hundred miles of Amaravati. After hearing Rudra's music the other night, the jaunty melody meant for dancing and carousing did not please Sati's ears. Vishwakarma had constructed the palace in such a way that it could accommodate thirty-three million devas, forty-eight thousand rishis and all of their attendants. Elaborate mazes wound through the halls of the palace.

As they exited from the palace to the Nandana gardens lined with sacred trees, Shachi darted forth to intercept them. She was vivacious, the curls of her hair framing her face as sensuously as the voluptuous curves that accentuated her slim body. Yellow silk cloth covered the lawn and on it were placed golden vessels filled with sweets: soft fudges, cottage cheese balls floating in sugared syrup, rose-flavoured milk, delicate cakes frosted in pink and blue, thick yoghurt sweetened with cardamom and jaggery. Hordes of apsaras giggled and danced across the forest groves, both to entertain and to be entertained.

Shachi squeezed each of them in a sisterly embrace, walking them out to join the other devis. After hugging Sati, Shachi drew back and admired the flower in her hair. She reached to touch it, but Sati shielded the flower with her palm.

Shachi planted her hands on her hips, her glittering bangles tinkling. The white filmy veil she wore over a crimson upper and lower cloth deepened the golden radiance of her complexion.

'Sati! Where did you find such a beautiful flower? You really won't let me touch it?'

Lakshmi laughed. 'Oh, Shachi! Don't even try. For the past so many days, Sati has had eyes only for that strange little flower. She is so protective of it, it stays in her hand even while she bathes, sleeps and eats. I have never seen her so obsessed.'

Shachi's eyes widened with interest. The other devis around them fell quiet, intrigued to hear more.

'Sati, where did you get it? It's so beautiful that I want one of my own, and clearly, you are not going to share yours.'

Sati was reluctant to say. Rudra would not like it if a horde of devis were to suddenly descend on his remote home at the edge of Mount Meru. She did not think he would offer them all flowers. Well, to be more precise, she hoped he would not.

Lakshmi winked at Sati. 'None other than Rudra—Mahadeva himself—gifted this flower to Sati.'

Titters of interest hummed around them.

Varuthini, one of the apsaras, exclaimed, 'Rudra! Isn't he far away in Kailash?'

Shachi leaned back against one of the trees, sipping from a tumbler of saffron milk. 'Oh, he is certainly in Mount Meru! Those hooligan *ganas* of his have been wreaking havoc. They even dared to break into Amaravati and tried to steal some of the soma! When the guards chased them out, they ran through the gardens, stomping over and ruining so many delicate shrubs.' She sighed in frustration. 'Well, at least they will be gone once the Night of Rudra is over.'

The Night of Rudra was just weeks away. Sati realised that she would not see Rudra for at least another year after that. She told herself she was relieved.

One apsara's voice dripped with disdain. 'Those *ganas* are nothing but ghastly monsters and rascals. How a deva, let alone someone who is called Mahadeva, can bear to be associated with such filthy beings is beyond me. Is he even a proper deva at all?'

Sati bristled with indignation. She wanted to defend Rudra. Before she could come up with a befitting reply, the currents of conversation had flowed elsewhere. They preferred comfortable topics, like dresses, food or the latest gossip about the *gandharvas* and apsaras who always fell into the most fascinating romances. The love stories of the devas were tame in comparison. When a couple was destined to be together—like Lakshmi and Narayana—they simply saw each other, knew they belonged to each other and immediately united. It had been a long time since there was a great love story between a deva and a devi.

They fed and drunk themselves full—for enjoyment rather than sustenance—then rested on soft satiny blankets for a nap in the sunshine. As Sati slept, she curved a hand protectively around the flower, nestling it against her heart, determined to keep it safe at all costs.

♋

A few days later, Sati was roused early in the morning by the appearance of Indra's *vahana*, Uchchaihshravas, the seven-headed, winged horse. Each deva and devi had their own *vahana*, typically a divine animal that served as their mount and companion.

The flapping of the horse's wings outside her window was so loud it woke Sati from a deep sleep. She rubbed her eyes and stared at Uchchaihshravas. His white coat was more radiant than the sun, his mane so luxurious and long that any woman would envy it. Each of his heads was coloured differently.

He neighed in a low tone, 'Devi, my mistress, Shachi, urgently needs your help and has sent me to fetch you.'

Sati sprang out of bed. She leapt onto the horse's broad back, gasping as he soared high into the skies, clinging to his mane so she would not fall off. In a trice, they were in Amaravati, and he whisked her directly to Shachi's private bedchamber. Sati's thoughts were in a riot. *Was there a new war with the asuras? Had Shachi fallen sick? Had she quarrelled terribly with Indra?*

Shachi was seated on a couch lined with pink velvet pillows. As Sati hurried to Shachi's side, she frowned, seeing Shachi's face drawn tight in worry, her hands wringing in her lap.

Sati sat by her side. 'What is wrong, dearest Shachi? I came as soon as I could.'

Shachi sighed deeply. 'Oh, Sati, I am in trouble!'

Sati hugged her tight. 'What is it? Tell me.'

Shachi placed a fluttering hand over her heart and sighed again. Sati braced herself to hear something truly terrible.

Shachi began timidly, 'Sati, remember when I told you that those hooligans of Rudra had come to create trouble and trampled across all my precious flowers?'

Sati nodded with a perplexed frown.

'Well... I saw how beautiful the flower was in your hair. And then I had an idea.'

A knot of worry tightened in Sati's belly. She remembered how greedily Shachi had eyed the flower in her hair.

'What did you do?' whispered Sati.

'I decided to get revenge, and I also wanted that flower so much, so, I took Uchchaihshravas and we went to Rudra's home in Mount Meru. I broke off a branch of the tree and brought it back here.'

Sati hissed in dismay. 'How could you? Didn't anyone stop you?'

Shachi shrugged. 'I don't think anyone was there. Anyway, when I told my husband about this, he was furious that I had dared to steal from Rudra. I thought it was just some flowers, why should he mind at all? But Indra is adamant that I make amends. Rudra's wrath is dangerous and can devour the entire world, he says. No one knows what could set him off.

'I promised Indra I would fix things. I figured, well, Rudra seems to have a soft spot for you, and you are always so good at smoothing things over, you know. So,

I thought you could help me.' She cast a hopeful glance at Sati.

Sati shook her head in anger. *How cruel and petty of Shachi.* Yet, Sati could never refuse anyone who approached her for help. On a table next to the couch, she saw a long dark-brown branch bearing half a dozen blossoms placed in a glass vase full of water. Her heart plummeted to see that the flowers had wilted brown.

Shachi's eyes followed Sati's gaze. 'I don't understand it, Sati. You've had the flower in your hair for a week and it's hardly aged a day. As soon as I plucked the branch, these flowers died.'

Sati rose, cradled the vase against her waist and inspected the flowers one by one. She said softly, sadly, 'These flowers are very special. You should not have treated them so carelessly.'

Shachi's ringed hands twisted together. Thick curls of hair fell over her ears as she looked up at Sati. 'You are so good at bringing things to life, Sati. Won't you please try to rescue the flowers and put them back in his home, so he doesn't start a war with Indra or do something terrible?'

For more than a day, Sati did nothing but concentrate on the flowers on the branch. She meditated to the depths of the white blossoms, searching for their source and root. At the heart of it all, she found an essence reminiscent of Rudra.

She traced the webbed veins of each petal. Their inner life force was intricately layered in tightly bound folds that pulsated with strength. The bewitching fragrance, something of sandalwood, myrrh and rose, had faded. She infused the petals with waves of life-sustaining energy. It exhausted her. She poured more of her vital force into it than she had on anything else.

After a day, the browning of the petals reversed, and they shone white as snow again. On the second day, the petals unfurled themselves into blooms once more, smaller and dimmer than before, but with a shadow of their earlier fragrance. Sati was delighted. Perhaps when they were back on the tree, they would grow properly.

At dusk, Sati walked to the edge of Mount Meru. There was a peculiar excitement in her, a thrill of anticipation and fear at perhaps once again meeting Rudra. Evening was falling when Sati reached his dwelling. She perched herself on the fence and used a special twine that she had blessed with many protective mantras to tie the branch back onto the tree. Dhanvantari had taught her how to do this, how to reassemble and mend broken plants and animals. In time, the twine would dissolve and the branch would be forged into the tree once again. Sati finished tying the knots. She bent the branch this way and that to test the strength of the twine.

Satisfied, she shimmied down the fence and brushed her yellow skirts clean. She exhaled in relief. It had actually worked. The flowers had been restored and Rudra had not discovered her. She could return home safely, having kept her promise to her friend.

She turned around and then jumped back to avoid colliding with Rudra. His arms were crossed over his chest, eyebrows knit together.

'Last time, you were stealing from my garden. This time, you appear to be leaving something behind.'

CHAPTER 4

Sati's cheeks reddened. 'Shachi saw the flower in my hair and liked it so much she wanted to take one of her own. She... she is really just too impulsive for her own good. She took a few flowers from here. She did not mean any harm. She asked me to help fix the flowers and bring them back to you.'

Well, it was mostly the truth. She left out Shachi's feelings about his *ganas*. Sati indicated with a wave of her hand the branch she had reattached. But Rudra's attention appeared to be focused on the tumult of curls in her hair, where the flower she had taken was tucked in with a golden pin.

Rudra leaned closer to inspect the flower, maintaining a respectful distance. For the first time, she allowed herself to look at him closely. His matted locks were reddish-black, and they fell across his broad shoulders in a chaotically beautiful way. From a loosely gathered top knot fell a rivulet of water, gathering and winding its way through his locks without ever escaping. It was the Ganga, the holiest of rivers, flowing through his hair.

When Ganga Devi had been commanded to descend to Earth, none could quell her rioting rage until Rudra took her into himself, placing her at the top of his head. As fierce and strong as the waters of the Ganga were, she now flowed placidly through his hair into all the worlds.

'I did not expect it to still be in your hair. Those flowers are meant to die quickly.' There was a note of surprise in his voice.

Sati touched the soft petals with pride. 'I worked hard to keep it safe.'

Rudra surveyed her dispassionately. 'You are a great devi. You should not become so attached to things that will not and cannot last.'

Sati could not reconcile the cold words with the sensitivity of the one who had brought the flowers to life, who had placed one in her hand, who played the veena so poignantly.

Her mouth fell open. 'I—I just wanted to take care of it, especially since you gave it to me.' Her cheeks pinkened. 'And, I wanted to help my friend. I wanted to correct the wrong she had done. I wanted to bring the flowers back to life. And I think I did!' She pointed again at the branch, hoping to distract him from the flower in her hair.

Rudra looked at the branch with a shake of his head. 'You should not have done that. She should not have broken the branch, but it was done. It cannot be undone.'

'But they are so beautiful. I have never seen flowers like these. How sad it would be if they were lost forever.' Perhaps the flowers had meant nothing at all to him.

Rudra turned away. 'They are not meant to last. One day, on a whim, I imagined such a thing and it came to be.

It was just that, a whim. A solitary thought, a fancy. And just as soon, I have forgotten it. It is *moha*, delusion, to try to make something, that cannot, last.'

Sati fell silent, clueless on how to respond.

Rudra said softly, 'I know it was not an easy thing to do. I know what you must have done to bring them back to life. You should have let them die.'

'Why?' The word tore out of her throat.

'Because death is not to be feared or dreaded. There is a rhythm to life and that includes death. Interrupting it is like interrupting a beautiful song. It disrupts the order of things. It is just a flower to you perhaps, but it is so much more than that. It is dangerous to play around with life and death if you do not have a proper understanding of these things.' Rudra turned to offer her a rueful smile. 'Never mind my words. You are a young girl yet.'

Now Sati's pride was hurt. She hissed, 'I am not a young girl! And I am not some idiot.' She scoffed, 'I understand life and death very well. Dhanvantari himself has taught me how to be a great healer. I can build entire worlds, you know. And Brhaspati says I could be a Mahadevi, just as you are Mahadeva. You do not know anything about me.'

Rudra said nothing but extended his arm, holding his hand out to her. There was a subtle challenge in the gesture. Sati promptly put her hand in his. His fingers slid down to her wrist, encircling them, and then pressed. It was like being branded, as if her bone and blood had ossified into thick blocks of ice. He tugged on her hand, and in an instant, she was transported with him to another world.

Everything was the colour of ash. The sea beneath their feet roiled, spewing out cold wisps of mist that wet their skin and clothes. The skies stormed and thundered. Gusts carrying saltwater and acidic rains lashed their skin. They stood on the jutted edge of a cliff. On one side was the roaring grey sea, on the other a yawning chasm of black nothingness. More than the physical elements, the pervasive desolation and isolation of this place terrified her.

When her eyes travelled to Rudra's face, she was shocked to see that he was in bliss. His head was flung back slightly, exposed to the wind, rain and sea, his eyes closed, trance-like. The mist from the sea and rain mingled with the fount of Ganga that he held at the top of his head. A *damaru* hung from his shoulder and swayed in rhythm with the wind, creating a staccato beat that thumped throughout the maelstrom, like a heartbeat.

Rudra's eyes slowly opened and the storm intensified. Eyes half-open, Rudra returned her gaze. For a moment, there was nothing but the locking of their gazes. The world became darker, stormier, uncontrolled. Rudra half-smiled. The wind keened in a high pitch, curdling Sati's blood. Tsunami-like waves of water lapped at the edge of the narrow rock promontory on which they stood. A bolt of lightning cracked. She shivered, and her feet slipped on the wet ground.

Rudra caught her forearms. His grip was like a vice, strong enough to leave a mark when he let go, a mark she would look at for days when this was over. He tugged her towards him and the sky, the world, the waters all vanished. Now there was only silence and darkness, a nothingness so pervasive that she could not remember her name. Sati looked around desperately, but it was as if she were blind, no, it was as if she had no eyes any more as if the sense of sight itself had disappeared. The form of Rudra had also disappeared, though she could still feel the press of his hands on her arms.

Still, there was that sense of expectancy, that he wanted something of her. But Sati could not think of what it was he wanted her to do or say. She felt afraid, more afraid here than she had in that harsh grey world. She opened her mouth to speak but there was no sound. There were only blankets of darkness and void. She pulled back from Rudra's grasp.

Immediately, he released her and they were back in his garden in Mount Meru. Sati took long, deep breaths, sucking in the air she was used to. Rudra's face was impassive, yet Sati saw a flicker of disappointment in his smouldering eyes.

Sati rubbed her arms, lacerated with cuts, the edges of her sari frayed from the sea and wind. The tattered pieces of the flower fell from her wet tangled hair, and she watched in dismay as they landed on the ground. How painstakingly she had taken care of the flower for weeks, and how pointlessly it had died.

'Why did you take me there?' Her voice quavered despite her best efforts.

Rudra crossed his arms over his chest. He watched as the remains of the flower fell to the ground as she combed her fingers through her hair.

His voice was as cool as the Ganga. 'It was a mistake. You are too young and naive, too obsessed with the surface of things. I misjudged you. It was wrong of me to take you.'

The emotionless delivery hurt Sati all the more deeply. Her eyebrows drew together in anger.

She stepped back from him. 'You are heartless and cruel,' she said. 'You have no regard for life.' It was unlike her to utter harsh words, and they emerged with more bark than bite.

Rudra smiled at her cryptically, a gleam of amusement sparkling in his dark eyes. 'And you have no regard for death.' He bent to pick up the pieces of the flower she had dropped, tucking them behind his ear. 'Everything and everyone is forgotten and abandoned in death. But in death, everything becomes precious to me. This is why I roam the cremation grounds and smear the ashes on my body, to honour those corpses left behind, to be their companion when everyone else has left. For those who have been abandoned, I will be there. This flower you tended so carefully, how quickly you discard it now that it has died. But I shall carry it with me forever. To love something, you must love it all the way through, even beyond death.' He paused as if he wanted to say more but then abruptly cut himself off. 'Leave now. It is getting late.'

Without another word, he turned around and walked away.

♋

Sati was a mess. She began stumbling on the path home. Salty tracks of dried tears roughened her cheeks. She could not remember feeling so disturbed. She had hardly walked five steps away from the fence when a majestic white bull soundlessly appeared next to her. He was beatific, self-illumined in the darkness of the evening. The same calmness that illumined Rudra's face shone in his.

As Sati walked, he matched her pace, his hooves crunching against the stone path. Sati watched him warily. 'I know who you are,' she announced. 'I know you are Nandi, the *vahana* of Rudra.'

He inclined his head proudly at the name of Rudra. Devas and their *vahanas* shared an unbreakable, unspoken bond. The *vahana* encapsulated the ethos and unique qualities of the deva. The *vahana* was the closest of associates, the best of devotees, the most loyal of companions. Sati sighed wistfully. She could not wait to have a *vahana* of her own.

Nandi trotted after her. She had to admit that his presence was comforting on what would have been a harrowing journey otherwise. She would have to tell Shachi that Rudra did not have a soft spot for her after all. But at least she had displaced any ill will from Rudra towards Shachi and redirected it to herself, however unintentionally. Waves of confusion and sadness coursed through her as she remembered that flicker of disappointment in his eyes, the coldness of his voice.

She felt as if she had failed at something important. But what? What was the point of being in that awful place where chaos and destruction reigned, where nothing else lived?

It made her head ache. She rubbed her temples and turned towards Nandi, determined to distract herself. 'How come I have never seen you before?'

Nandi angled his head in Rudra's direction. He appeared to be as taciturn as his master. Sati guessed he meant he was always following the footsteps of Rudra.

Sati sighed. 'It is a long walk back home, and I have had a hard day. The least you could do is give me some good company.'

Nandi regarded her as warily as she had regarded him a few minutes earlier. Then he half snorted, half sighed and edged closer to her, until his flank was pressed against her leg. She stared at him uncomprehendingly. He nudged her hard enough that she tipped over and ended up sitting on his back. Then he charged forth, hurtling down the path.

In a blur of movement and whooshing sounds, they reached the front entrance of Sati's home. Sati got off his back shakily, brushing the dust off her yellow sari, running her hands through her tousled hair. Nandi, however, was not breathless after moving at that breakneck pace.

Sati reached out with a tentative hand and petted his ears affectionately. Nandi allowed it with a dip of his head, ever majestic and proud in his stance.

'It was very kind of you to bring me home,' she said. She could not help but think that he was much nicer than Rudra, who had rudely cast her away. It burned a hole in her heart remembering how he had spoken to her at the end.

Nandi watched her with a severe gaze. In a stiff, stentorian voice, he proclaimed, 'I only go where Rudra sends me.'

And with that, he, too, turned around and walked away.

♋

Lakshmi and Saraswati were distraught to see Sati in such a state.

Lakshmi exclaimed, 'Sati, what happened? Were you in a fight? Did you get hurt?'

Saraswati wrapped Sati in a blanket and brought her soothing rose tea that she had brewed herself with secret herbs designed to calm the nerves.

Sati sank into the soft red velvet sofa next to her sisters. 'I was gravely insulted,' she said in a despondent tone.

Lakshmi and Saraswati looked at each other in surprise. No one dared to insult Sati. No one could say an unkind word to her. She was too beautiful, too sweet, too kind. She was everyone's favourite. She never lost her temper or acted arrogantly. It was unthinkable that anyone in Mount Meru would be harsh to her. Even her father, the volatile Daksha, was indulgent towards her.

Lakshmi squeezed Sati's hands while Saraswati refilled her tumbler of tea. In a gentle voice, Lakshmi asked, 'What happened, dearest?'

Sati's eyes narrowed. 'He called me young. And foolish. And selfish.' *Well, not exactly in those many words, but that had been the overall meaning,* Sati told herself.

Lakshmi muttered an invocation under her breath. In a poof of blue smoke, Narayana appeared across the table, reclining on the couch across from them. He seemed to have been napping from wherever he had come; as he sat up, he stretched his arms with a yawn and looked at Lakshmi.

His lotus-shaped eyes shone affectionately as he asked, 'Lakshmi? Why did you call me here? Have you been missing me?' His tone was flirtatious.

Lakshmi harrumphed. 'Do not flatter yourself, husband. I have called you here in an emergency.'

He was at once intent and alert, though his expression did not alter.

'What is it?' His voice was sharp and urgent.

Lakshmi stiffened her spine. 'Someone dared to insult Sati.'

Narayana's gaze shifted to Sati, his eyes widening in surprise. 'Who dared to insult my sister-in-law?'

Sati took a long sip of tea as she considered how to respond. She had wanted to vent to her sisters but not cause trouble.

Lakshmi's voice turned ominous. 'They said she was young. And foolish. And selfish.'

Narayana's eyes widened in surprise, creasing the sandalwood *tilakam* in the centre of his forehead. 'Sati?'

Lakshmi inclined her head in confirmation, her golden earrings swaying.

'Who?' Narayana asked.

All heads turned toward Sati.

'Rudra,' she whispered. As always, merely saying his name pinkened her cheeks.

Now they all looked at her in astonishment.

'Rudra?' sputtered Lakshmi. 'But he's the one who gave you that flower!'

Saraswati patted her arm. 'I did tell you to be careful of him, dear.'

Narayana chuckled, a slow smile spreading across his face. He leaned back against the cushions and studied Sati, waiting for her to say more. But she did not want to share the details. As unpleasant as the experience had been, it belonged only to Rudra and her.

Lakshmi glared at her husband. 'Well, are you going to do something about this or not?'

Narayana kept his gaze on Sati. Her eyes trailed to the Sudarshana Chakra whirling above his right index finger.

As always, it discomfited her. She imagined the serrated edges cutting into her flesh. Her fear was ridiculous— how could Narayana ever be her enemy? But it was a feeling she could not shake off.

'Indeed, my dear,' Narayana said softly, 'if Rudra disrespected Sati, it cannot be ignored. Do not worry. I will have a word with him.'

♋

Narayana came to see Rudra at midnight, which he knew was Rudra's favourite hour. When others slept, Rudra was awake and meditating. When the night-roving rakshasas prowled the lands, he was at the height of his powers.

No one else would have disturbed him at this time. But Narayana walked into the house and sat down across from Rudra, who was staring at a fire as it slowly dwindled into embers.

Rudra did not meet Narayana's eyes. 'What are you doing here?'

Narayana snorted. 'Good to see you, too, brother, after a few thousand years.'

Rudra's lips twitched into a smile. 'You have been spending too much time in the mortal realms, brother. What seems thousands of years to you has just been one year here.'

'It feels like it has been a long time.'

Rudra nodded. It was always like this between them. A moment could have passed or a millennium, but the dynamic of their relationship never changed.

Rudra grabbed a brass tumbler and filled it with an unidentified liquid, handing it to Narayana.

Narayana peered at it from a distance. 'Do I want to know what it is?'

Rudra tilted his head back, exposing his neck to the glow of the firelight. At the base of his throat was a deep blue mark. When the milky ocean had been churned, producing the vile Halahala that was poisoning all the worlds and living creatures, Rudra had drunk it and kept it in his throat without swallowing, taking the pain and suffering unto himself and saving the universe. He was the only one capable of imbibing the poison without being destroyed.

Narayana smiled. 'Very well. You do like to rub it in how you saved us from the Halahala. We have not forgotten, brother. I shall drink whatever it is you have given me.' It was a white, milk-like substance with some rare herbs that were faintly intoxicating. *It was pleasant after all*, ruminated Narayana. He drank deeply from the tumbler and vowed to get the recipe.

With a sigh, Narayana turned to the matter at hand. 'I understand you have grievously insulted my sister-in-law.'

'You mean, Sati, the daughter of Daksha Prajapati?' At Narayana's nod, Rudra scoffed. 'Hardly. I was just being honest with her. She is too sensitive for her own good.'

'She is very sweet. She is one of the most accomplished and powerful devis. I was surprised to hear that you were rude to her.'

Rudra diverted the topic. 'So, now Lakshmi has sent you to scold me, has she?'

Narayana's jaw tightened. 'I am not here to scold you. And I did not come because of my wife. Well, not just because of her. I really am very fond of Sati and do not like to see her upset. It seems... there is something between you two and whatever you said or did affected her deeply. You need to make it right.'

Rudra refolded his legs under him, straightening his torso. He was of a magnificent height, broad in chest and shoulders. As his shadow leapt across the walls, the silhouette of the snake slung around his neck shone dark against the fire-illumined wood of the hut. With his halo of wild hair and smouldering eyes glowing red in the firelight, he truly looked the part of Mahadeva, the greatest of the great devas.

'She annoyed me,' Rudra admitted reluctantly.

Narayana smiled. 'You? The great yogi? The ascetic one who is immovable, unshakeable, eternally indifferent? That sweet girl annoyed you?'

Rudra snorted. 'Must you always be so poetic and exaggerated in speech? It is rather irritating.' He turned his gaze back to the fire and shrugged. 'I misjudged her. I thought there was more to her than just... prettiness and flowers. I thought there was depth.'

Narayana was perplexed. 'No one has ever accused Sati of being superficial.'

'Of course not. That's not what I meant. She is too caring and kind for her own good. One day, it will get her into trouble. I just thought...' Rudra was uncharacteristically at a loss for words. 'There was a flower. The way she touched it and held it, I had hope. That she was my match. That she could understand me, perhaps even appreciate me. But, in reality, I terrify her, as I should.'

Narayana was delighted. Recently wed, he was looking forward to seeing Rudra get married soon, too.

It had seemed impossible to find someone who would be up to Rudra's standards.

Narayana used his most encouraging tone of voice. 'You must give her a little bit of time, brother. She has not even chosen her *vahana* yet. She is a girl, not fully a woman. Let her grow up a bit. Be patient with her. I think she will make you very happy in times to come.'

Rudra rolled his eyes. 'Just because you got trapped, do not drag me down with you. Anyway, it is finished. It is best if I never see her again. She can forget me and not feel upset any more. Let her be comfortable and happy in her world.'

Narayana set down the tumbler firmly. 'No, no. Even if you are not interested in her, you must not let things end this way. You do not want to be on the wrong side of her or her father. Or my wife, for that matter. Just apologise to her or send her a token of your regard, something conciliatory.'

Rudra downed the rest of his drink. 'That is your problem, Narayana. You always get enmeshed in the lives of others, caring about their feelings and how to keep things smooth and harmonious. You do not even get the time to properly meditate, always hopping from one avatar to another, meddling in human affairs. It is ceaseless, thankless labour, getting involved with others. I prefer to go to the root of the problem and tear it out. The problem is I unsettle Sati, and therefore the best solution is to avoid her completely. An apology or some such silly thing just masks the underlying issue and prolongs the problem. No, Narayana, I have decided. There will be no further interaction. Anyway, in a few days, after my yajna has ended, I shall go back to Kailash. Then all this will be resolved naturally.'

Narayana smiled. It was the longest string of words he had heard from Rudra. He was protesting a bit too much. Narayana stood to leave and put a hand on Rudra's shoulder.

'Do not overthink it, brother. Do not leave her upset. Make it right.'

With that he departed, leaving Rudra scowling into the dying fire in the depths of the black night.

CHAPTER 5

A few days later, Sati was resting in the late afternoon. Her father, Daksha, walked into her chamber and took her hand.

'Come, daughter. It is the Night of Rudra. You must join us tonight.'

It was the fourteenth day of the dark fortnight of Magha, the Night of Rudra. From dawn, an eerie silence had taken over all of Mount Meru. Everyone, including the *vahanas*, was solemnly fasting. Even the *gandharvas* and apsaras had abandoned the celestial gardens, retreating into isolation. There were other festival days on which there was general merriment, laughter and the smells of cooking and flower decorations enriched the air. This one day of the year was sombre. None dared to smile. All walked slowly, eyes downcast, lips moving soundlessly to the repetition of Rudra's name.

Daksha waited as she tied her hair. 'Perhaps this will be a good distraction for you. You have been moping so much lately.'

'I have not been moping!' The truth was, though, she had been in a foul mood since her last encounter with

Rudra. She shivered in dread at facing him today. There would be millions of celestials in attendance, so perhaps he would not notice her.

Sati dressed in a pale-yellow sari with no ornaments. It was not a night for jewellery or gems. Rudra brought out the asceticism in the devas.

They walked slowly to the assembly hall. Sati remembered that moment on the mountaintop, with the howling of the wind and the churning of the sea, all that energy in action. Now all of that kinetic frenzy stilled into a thick silence that blanketed Mount Meru. The wind did not move. Not a single leaf fell from a tree branch.

Even Daksha was unusually mute, his eyes flitting this way and that as they walked, as if Rudra would pounce on him for not behaving properly. He made it a point to mutter the mantra of Rudra audibly as if to prove his devotion. Sati smiled wryly at that.

They entered the assembly hall. Rows of *ganas* took the customary place of the principal devas. Between Rudra and the *ganas* roared a gigantic sacrificial fire into which were poured incessant streams of offerings—ghee, herbs, scented wood, honeyed sweets—causing the flames to sputter and sparkle in different colours. The drone of the Vedic chants and the mantras invoking and placating the formidable Rudra made the marble floor and the gilded walls vibrate.

Daksha took his officiating place next to the fire. Sati looked for an empty seat. The only vacant spot appeared to be right in the front, near the fire and her father. She sank to her feet to sit cross-legged on the floor.

She tried to meditate but could not take her eyes off Rudra. He sat on a golden throne, covered with a tiger skin, one emerald-green cobra coiled on the gilded edge of the throne behind his neck. At his side were his *trishula*, the gleaming trident, and the *damaru*. At his feet sat the majestic Nandi, watching the crowd with half-hooded eyes. Rudra's eyes were closed, his body motionless, deep in trance.

His body was the colour of a stormy sea, a grey-white-green hue. The rivulets of the Ganga flowed over him, bathing him tenderly, and she felt suddenly jealous of the great river. His hands rested lightly on his lap. His face was etched like stone, a faint smile playing at the edges of his lips, dark red against the pale skin of his face. When Sati could not bear any longer the splendour of his face, her eyes travelled to his hair. It was loose and untamed, more luxurious than the mane of a lion, more beautiful than black silk. It was red and black and golden all at once, exposed to and reflecting the elements of sun, wind, fire and desert air. It was elemental. He was elemental.

Sati peered into the fire pit. She could see all the mortals in all the worlds paying obeisance to Rudra. Thieves called out to him as the lord of thieves. Hunters called out to him as the lord of the hunters. Traders called out to him as the chief of traders. And so did the fishermen. Cowherds, women carrying water from wells, all the creatures of the forests and plains and seas called out to him. Even the plants undulated their leaves and dropped blossoms as offerings to him. On the cremation grounds, in the mountain caves, in the forests under millions of trees, Rudra was worshipped by all.

Sati looked at Rudra again as night fell. Around her, most of the devas had fallen into deep meditation. Sati still could not bring herself to close her eyes. The shadows lengthened on the walls, and then, transformed into forms of Rudra. In some, his throat was black and in some it was white. In some, his hair was matted and he was bearded, in others he was clean-shaven. He was visible inside dark thunder clouds and in the lightning, too. He glittered in the clouds and mingled with the rain and sunshine. He appeared in the deep waters and in the dew drops. He was hidden in the thorny dense forests and yet stood always before those who were his devotees. His arms carried thousands of weapons. Yet his face remained peaceful and compassionate, the planes of his face smooth and radiant.

At the edges of her consciousness, Sati could just about make out the roar of the wind and the sea that she had heard when they stood on the mountainside. Yet, hearing it now, there was something beyond aversion that pulled at her. She found herself standing up and walking towards Rudra. She was pulled by that force, like a moth to a flame.

This was not the fire that would burn her; it was the one that would make her alive. Deep in his trance, Rudra was oblivious to her. She could smell the offerings being heaped at his feet and offered into the fire—the sandalwood paste, the scented milk, the fruit juice, the copious amounts of clarified butter. From his body emanated a subtle, elegant scent that she recognised from the white flower he had given her. She sank to her knees before him, and finally, so overwhelmed was she that her eyes fell closed.

And she was back on that mountainside, amid the storm and sea and wind, and he was right there in front of her. This time she did not hesitate to fall into his arms, to sink into his embrace. She felt the whirlwind around them but now she was in the centre of it with him. His arms around her were cold and warm all at once, like ice and fire melted together. She had become boneless, and the more she melted into him, the tighter he held her. Even as the world swirled into a frenzy around them, in their embrace, there was only stillness and silence. When the cold, the wet, the biting wind made her shiver, he enveloped her protectively, holding her hard against him. And then there was nothing at all, only the beginning of bliss.

As they stood like that, for moments, perhaps, or for hours, something began to unfurl within her, something that responded to his icy calm. If he was grey and white, a large wave of red petals blossomed deep within her, like the rippling of silk. It spread from her belly to her heart to her head and legs, every inch of her. It was blinding light and nourishing heat; it was the movement of life. It was a surge of something so powerful and fierce that she repressed it with a shudder, afraid that it would break her apart.

'Sati! Be careful of the fire!'

Rudra's voice snapped her back to reality. She had somehow fallen back, dangerously close to the fire pit. Rudra leaned forward and pulled her with one arm toward him until she tumbled onto his tiger-skin-covered lap, sitting on his left leg. She blushed a deep scarlet. Everyone knew that sitting on a man's left leg was reserved for a wife or lover. The right leg was for daughters and grandchildren. But he did not let her go.

He stared at her stormily. 'I do not like to see you so close to the fire. You could have fallen in.'

She breathed in the musky fragrance of him, the combination of the ashes and that old white flower. As Sati shifted, only slightly uncomfortable, on Rudra's lap, the serpent slung around his neck, a signifier that he had conquered death, slithered away politely and respectfully, to Sati's great relief. She felt an irresistible urge to touch Rudra's hair and lifted her hand to do so. But his eyes had fallen half-closed, and he was again lost in meditation. How gentle his arm was around her waist. *Rudra*. She said his name to herself. It felt incomplete.

Sati gazed into his half-open eyes and whispered, 'Shiva,' just as the gong sounded midnight and the chanting reached a fevered pitch. The word just slipped out. It meant that which was auspicious.

Rudra's eyes flew open. Her adoring gaze was locked on his face. 'Shiva,' she repeated with more conviction. 'You are not just Rudra. You are Shiva.'

He bent his head downward in acknowledgment, sombre.

'*Tathastu*,' he said. *So be it*.

She felt faint. Her body grew slack in his arms, and he beckoned Nandi over to their side. He gently placed Sati on Nandi's back and instructed him to carry her home safely. The last thing Sati saw before her eyes closed sleepily and her head fell limply against Nandi's warm flesh was Shiva resuming his lotus pose. He once more went into a deep trance that would last the rest of the night.

♋

Sati woke late the next afternoon. In her dreams, she felt Shiva's arms around her—yes, that's how she thought of him now, as Shiva. And it was such a delectable feeling that she was loath to wake up until Lakshmi and Saraswati came into her chamber.

Sati stretched and sighed with a yawn. 'I'm having such a pleasant slumber, why must you disturb me?'

Her two sisters exchanged looks. 'Well, Narayana is here to see you. So, you better get ready and come out fast,' said Saraswati.

Sati covered her head with a pillow. 'Oh, can't you tell him to come later? I am so very sleepy.'

Lakshmi said slyly, 'That's too bad. He brought you a gift from Ru—Shiva. I guess now you will have to wait to see it.'

At that, Sati jumped out of bed and hurriedly dressed behind a screen. 'Has everyone started calling him Shiva?' It made her smile that her name for him had caught on.

'Oh, yes. It is quite mysterious. It seems sometime around midnight, a voice whispered out "Shiva". And it carried so much force, so much conviction, that even the rishis broke out of meditation. They had never heard a name said with so much love and devotion. Shiva himself said *tathastu*. And the rest of the night, all the rishis, all the devas, all the mortals, all the ones who worshipped him started saying "Om Namah Shivaya". The mortals were especially happy because this was so much easier to say than all that complicated Vedic chanting. And Shiva himself enjoyed it so much that he decreed it his favourite mantra, which means Shiva is now his favourite name.'

Sati turned a deep red.

Lakshmi's eyes sparkled in amusement as she teased her. 'And did you know, Sati, that the voice at midnight was the soft sound of a devi who happened to be sitting in Shiva's embrace?'

Sati tied her hair into a loose bun and dashed out of the room to avoid having to finish that conversation. She rushed to the sitting room, where her brother-in-law was waiting. Suddenly, a lion cub leapt in front of her and roared angrily. Sati nearly jumped out of her skin.

Narayana snatched the cub by the scruff of its neck and took it back into his arms, pacifying him with a soothing murmur. He addressed a horrified Sati, 'He never makes things easy, does he?'

Sati knew he was talking about Shiva. She pointed at the lion reluctantly. 'Shiva left that for me?'

Narayana inclined his head. 'He left Mount Meru this morning and will not be back for a long time. He asked me to give this to you.'

She peered at the lion who was stretching out his paws, straining to evade Narayana's arms. 'Is it a pet of his that he wants me to take care of while he is away?'

Narayana shook his head. 'I've never seen this creature before.'

Sati knelt on the floor and waved her arms in confusion. 'What do I do with him? He's wild and untamed, fierce and dangerous.'

As her hands fluttered nervously, the cub wriggled out of Narayana's arms and paced over to her, nuzzled her hand and lay his head on her lap with a low, demanding growl.

Narayana smiled. 'Perhaps just accept him and give him your affection.'

Sati understood that neither of them was talking about the cub.

Saraswati and Lakshmi joined them. Lakshmi wondered out loud, 'Perhaps he left the lion behind to protect Sati?'

Sati sighed in exasperation. 'Protect me from what? I have no enemies and there is no danger in my life.'

The four of them stared at the lion, mystified at the meaning of Shiva's gift.

♋

One day, Narayana was reclining on the back of Shesha, the *nagaraja* or the king of the nagas, and Brahma was sitting at his feet. They were resting in the Ksheera Sagara.

Brahma examined his fingernails as he said in a bored voice, 'Daksha Prajapati has petitioned to meet with the three of us.' It was a reference to Brahma, Narayana and Shiva—the trinity of the Creator, the Preserver and the Destroyer, respectively. Only matters of cosmic importance were deemed worthy of their collective attention.

Narayana made a humming noise in his throat. 'Really? I wonder what weighs so heavily on his mind.' He smiled as if he already knew the answer and closed his eyes again. With every breath, he exhaled worlds into creation.

After a short time, Daksha Prajapati approached in formal obeisance. He sang hymns in praise of Narayana. Although he bowed respectfully to Brahma, he did not recite any hymns for him. Once, Brahma had angered Shiva, and as punishment, Shiva had decreed the prohibition of all worship of Brahma. He retained his official role as the Creator, but Brahma was subservient to both Narayana and Shiva. Narayana waved his hand for Daksha to rise, who then sat at their feet.

Brahma asked, 'Shall we wait for Shiva?'

Narayana half-smiled. 'Shiva will appear if and when he wants to appear. Tell us what is on your mind, Daksha.'

'It is time for Sati to get married. She has become quiet and withdrawn these past few weeks. I worry about her. She is no ordinary devi, as you know. Her marriage concerns all the immortals and all the worlds. Only if the match is right will there be peace and blessings across the universe. So, I have come to consult you on who the right husband for my daughter would be.'

At that moment, Shiva appeared in a flash of white light. He sat cross-legged atop a tiger skin mat, hovering above the milky waters.

Narayana chuckled. 'You always do know the right time to show yourself, Shiva.'

Daksha's lips curled downward, as though displeased at Shiva's arrival. Shiva did not bother with any greetings, save a deep and impenetrable stare directed towards Daksha. 'Have you asked Sati whether she wants to get married?'

Daksha's face, with his puffed cheeks and shaggy white beard, flushed red. 'I am her father. I know what is best for her.'

Shiva's voice roughened with disapproval. 'She has not even had her *vahana* ceremony yet. Her identity and personality have yet to be settled. You cannot marry her off until she knows herself.'

Daksha felt his anger simmer and silently implored Narayana and Brahma to rescue the conversation.

Narayana broke in diplomatically, 'Since we are all here, share your thoughts with us, Daksha.'

Daksha stroked his beard in contemplation. 'My daughter is of a sweet, gentle and refined disposition. And she needs the same qualities in her husband. I have gone through all the eligible devas and only two suitable matches came to mind.'

Narayana sat up in interest. 'Do tell.' His voice crackled with amusement. Shiva sat as immobile as marble.

'At first, I considered Dhanvantari. He is the medicinal sage among the devas and a healer par excellence. He is worshipped by all vaidyas, who are mortal healers and medical practitioners. He is the master of all herbs and therapies. He and Sati would be a natural match.'

Daksha plucked one hair from his beard and held it up. It slowly transformed into a purple bubble, in which the four of them could see a vision of Sati's life with Dhanvantari. They roamed the forests, picking herbs for medicines and writing medical texts together. They lived in a simple hut near a babbling brook. Sati looked content.

Shiva pierced the bubble with the dagger of his glance. 'Preposterous,' he uttered dismissively.

Narayana coughed and hid a smile behind his hand. Daksha glowered but continued, 'Well, the second one may be an even better match. Kamadeva, the deva of love and romance.'

Shiva rolled his eyes as Daksha conjured a pink bubble that showed the new potential couple. Kamadeva was the matchmaker among the devas, the arranger of love stories. It was no wonder that in this vision he regaled Sati with the most romantic of poetry, gifted her with elaborate wreaths of flowers and played soft, sweet lullabies for her in the evening. Shiva burst that bubble even more quickly.

Daksha shrank back as Shiva muttered through gritted teeth, 'Totally ridiculous.' He took a deep breath and said contemptuously, 'You do not know the worth of your daughter. They are not qualified to be matched with her.'

Daksha cast his eyes downward in assent. 'Yes, you are right. That is actually why I have come today. Of the thirty-three million devas, I do not see one capable of being her match. I am perhaps a doting father, but it is the truth. Brahma-deva, I have come to beseech you to act once more as the Creator and create from your mind a new deva, one who is fit to be Sati's husband.'

Before Brahma could reply, Shiva put up his hand to stop him. He turned a cold stare at Daksha, no longer casual. His eyes grew stormy grey and his voice was glacial. 'Stop this foolishness, Daksha. Her marriage is not your concern. And it is beyond Brahma's capabilities to create one equal to her.'

Daksha had no choice but to retreat. But he was not ready to give up yet, not by a long shot.

CHAPTER 6

Six months had passed since the Night of Rudra, and Sati's *vahana* ceremony was approaching. It was the new source of excitement for all the celestials in Mount Meru. Daksha had decided to hold the ceremony as soon as possible. He was eager to get Sati married. He wanted a prince among the devas for his daughter, partly for Sati's happiness but also because he wanted his daughter and son-in-law to eclipse even Lakshmi and Narayana in glory. That ambition kept growing in him, although he knew it to be unvirtuous.

While the Night of Rudra had been austere and sombre, Sati's *vahana* ceremony was a celebration. Rose petals carpeted all the walking paths. Musicians and bards crowded the lawns to entertain the divine guests. Apsaras danced chastely. The sky glowed a rosy pink shade.

Sati was the only one not in a celebratory mood. She was nervous. This was a significant moment, one that would determine her destiny as a devi. It was her rite into adulthood. And she still did not know who she was.

Sati wondered if Shiva would come. It was irrational to expect him. He was at Kailash, deep in meditation, and he rarely came to Mount Meru. Of course, he had been invited by Daksha, who was too afraid to insult him. But no one expected him to be there.

It took several hours for Sati to get ready. Her sisters helped her bathe in rose-scented milk, in perfumed lukewarm water and then in sandalwood-scented honeyed water. She was dressed in an effervescent pink sari, set off against a dark green upper cloth. Her hair was tied into two elaborate braids pinned to the centre of her head. Her skin was exfoliated with Himalayan pink salts until it shimmered, smooth as a pearl. Her toenails were painted a ruby red.

She wore anklets, toe rings, finger rings, bracelets that chimed together sweetly with every flick of her wrist and a golden waist belt. Every piece of jewellery was inlaid with the finest of gems—emeralds, rubies, diamonds. Lakshmi and Saraswati regarded her in awe.

They escorted her to the assembly hall. Before leaving, Sati beckoned her lion. She had never named him. They had grown so intimate that she did not even need to call to him. As soon as she thought of him, he appeared. He was silent and grave, yet utterly powerful and fierce. In the past few months, the cub had grown into a full lion. He ate only from her hand. If anyone approached him, he would snarl at them menacingly, sending them running.

He accompanied her on walks through the dense forests, waited patiently when she climbed trees or walked into faraway galaxies and then carried her home proudly on his back. He slept at the foot of her bed. She often fell asleep with her hand nestled into his mane.

'I better not take you with me today,' she whispered. He was liable to scare the others in the assembly hall. But she did not want him to get bored at home. 'Why don't you roam around in the mortal worlds and I'll see you in the morning?' The lion trotted off obediently.

The three devis entered the assembly hall, side by side. All the celestials turned to her with admiring smiles, many sighing in appreciation of her beauty. A golden throne with a red velvet seat had been specially prepared for her by Daksha. He stood next to it, his chest swelled with pride as he watched his daughter walk up to him.

She made her way slowly, gracefully. A crown of rare red roses—from a valley in a faraway world, uninhabited by sentient beings—lay atop her head. She had woven it herself. She took her father's hand as she sat cross-legged on the seat.

Daksha took his place among the celestials. Her two sisters sat on lotus thrones on either side of her.

Agni Deva, with a flick of his fingers, lit all the lamps in the assembly hall. The sky outside darkened into evening, so that only the light of the lamps illumined the interior. He then bowed to Sati.

It was time to start. Sati took a deep breath and blinked slowly. In front of her stood a horde of animals from which she could pick her *vahana*—peacocks, cattle of different hues, all sorts of exotic birds. First, though, she had to go into a meditative state. Only then could she choose the right one.

Not a peep sounded in the assembly hall. She closed her eyes and listened to the crackling of the flames of the sacrificial fire burning in her honour. In the space of a few moments, she felt Lakshmi and Saraswati filling her with their energies. Gradually, she fell into a deep meditation. She could feel the strength of the thirty-three million devas and devis surrounding her, supporting her.

She inhaled and exhaled rhythmically. The further inward she withdrew, the more she expanded across the universe, feeling light and warmth radiate outward from within her belly.

Yet, her heart hammered. She was unmoored, restless. The devas waited for her expectantly. It usually did not take more than a few minutes for this part of the process to finish. But, more than an hour had passed and she still could not rouse herself. There was something missing. She thought of that world she had built and presented to her guru, what he had said to her about balance and opposites. She thought of the look in Shiva's eyes when she had pulled away from him. There was something she had not yet learned. Without that, she was afraid to open her eyes, to choose her *vahana*, to make a mistake that would affect the rest of her existence. She wondered in a panic if the ceremony was taking place too soon. Maybe she was not yet ready. Maybe she was not qualified. Her palms began to sweat. She wanted to run away.

And then she heard the light patter of his bare feet in the assembly hall. Her eyes jerked open and she stared at Shiva. All anxiety and fear left her. Time slowed and stopped. One of his names was Kaal Bhairava, the Lord of Time. He walked slowly and stood before her.

Never had anyone looked as beautiful to Sati as he did. He was majestic and calm, radiant and overflowing with power. At that moment, she lost her heart to him. He took her in with soft affection, the same way he had looked at the white flower after it had fallen to the ground from her hands. His glance was so warm that she began to feel dizzy.

Shiva slanted his head in a request for permission. She nodded. She remembered how she had named him Shiva that night. In some way, she had completed him, and now it was his turn to do the same for her.

He knelt at her feet. He reached out his hand to hold her right foot. His touch sent a jolt of electricity through her, and she would have jumped out of her seat had he not gripped her foot. He let her left foot remain crossed but pulled her right foot down to touch the ground. As soon as the tender bottom of her foot made contact with the cold ground, a rush of energy coursed downward from the tip of her head to the sole of her right foot, pouring into the ground, blessing all the worlds.

She closed her eyes and felt the power, shakti—the life force that sustained the entire universe—flowing through her like a river in spate. She opened her eyes again to see that the pink of her sari had deepened into crimson red, the red of blood and fire and life itself. The red of womanhood. Her braids had loosened into waves that cascaded down her back, black as night.

Shiva's eyes darkened as he looked at her. She could not know how enchanting, how captivating she was at that moment. Any deva whose eyes had opened would have fallen in love with her in a heartbeat, but Shiva did not let anyone else awaken.

He lifted the crown of flowers from her head. He held it until it grew into a circlet of gold. The roses transformed into rubies that retained their shape and colour but were now brighter than the sun. This crown would last forever, unlike the simple one she had designed. He carefully placed it back on her head.

He leaned back and studied her, inch by inch. She watched him wide-eyed. It was as if he was not completely satisfied, as if the dress, the decorations, did not do her justice. Even the golden crown he had fashioned did not appear to placate him.

Then, with a sudden movement, he plucked out the crescent moon that adorned his hair and tucked it carefully into Sati's, behind the golden crown. The moon, cold as it was, still bore the warmth of his body, the inner fire of his *tapasya*, and she felt the accumulated powers of thousands of years of meditation flow from Shiva to her. It was more intimate than an embrace. His fingers sifted through her hair, sliding across her scalp in a way that made her flesh tingle. As brightly as the moon shone, it paled in comparison to the radiance emanating from her now that she was in her full power.

For a moment, his hand lingered in her hair. She wished that the wheel of time would never again continue its rotations, that time would remain frozen in this moment forever.

Then, in the space of a moment, everything changed.

♋

Her lion howled. Not the angry, proud roar that she was used to but a howl of pain and fear. All the way from the mortal realms, the sound reverberated into Sati's being, and with a gasp, her reverie broke. Desperate to reach his side, she dashed out of the assembly hall, pushing open the heavy doors with the might of her mind.

There was so much sheer power coursing through her that she could not contain herself. Her limbs shook.

She moved faster than the wind. She came to the edge of the mountain and peered down into the abyss below. The mortal realms were somewhere in the darkness, millions of miles below the base of Mount Meru.

Sati rarely visited the mortal worlds, but now she was pulled to her lion's side, desperate to save him. He roared again in agony as if he were close to death. Her hearing had become superfine, and even as she prepared to leap over the mountainside, down into the murky darkness of the mortal realms below, she heard the thudding of twin pairs of footsteps behind her.

She felt Shiva reach for her arm to restrain her, as he urgently called out, 'Sati, come back! He is safe. I will bring him back.'

But there was something elemental in her that propelled her feet into thin air, hurtling her down at the speed of light, an urge to save, to protect one of her own. She jumped, not knowing where she was going, determined to reach her companion. With the power of her will alone, she found her lion. He was lying in a forest in one of the millions of mortal words created by Narayana, badly wounded by a hunter's arrow.

This was a world she had not seen before. It was dimly lit, as if there were no sun in the sky, only little flickers of light beaming up from the tough grass that gave the air a dull yellow glow. She shuddered with distaste as she smelled spilled blood—of her lion and the humans who had done this to him.

Shiva and Narayana landed lightly on their feet behind her. She did not have to look back to know that they were there. No object of knowledge was hidden from her. She could see everything, be anywhere, do anything.

She placed her hand on the lion and winced. She felt his pain as her own as if her flesh had been torn asunder, her blood leaching out onto the ground. Tears fell from her eyes onto his fur, and the lion was instantly healed. The hunters, and now she could see there were dozens of them encircling her, drew closer, their bows primed to shoot at her.

Shiva clasped her elbow and spoke into her ear. 'Come, Sati, let's go back.'

She could not bring herself to leave. She could still feel her lion's pain through his ragged breathing, and it drove her mad. Suffering and cruelty were alien to her, unbearable. She held her hands out, and a sword appeared in her right hand and a ball of fire in her left. Before Shiva or Narayana could react, she threw the fireball at the hunters, and they screamed in agony and rushed at her. She swung her sword across furiously. Within a second, they had all fallen dead, staining her bare feet red from the gore that flowed. As the blood dripped from the edge of her sword, her mouth salivated. Her tongue elongated, stretching towards that salty, acrid spot of blood.

Narayana and Shiva stood before her protectively. Narayana stepped in to stop her bloodlust, intent to carry her back to Devaloka. Her hand tightened on the sword. She was not ready to go back. Shiva halted him with a raised hand, his eyes never leaving Sati's face. He looked at her with intensity, with desire.

Sati could see the hunters and rakshasas arrayed behind Shiva and Narayana. It was not just her lion that had been hurt. They were terrorising the mortal beings who inhabited this planet, burning down villages, raping and plundering. And now she could feel each shudder of fear, each cry of anguish and each death as if they were wracking her own being. It almost brought her to her knees, but an even stronger force held her upright. She was invincible. Her strength was adamantine, her determination ruthless.

She had never known suffering, her own or anyone else's. And she would not tolerate it. She charged forward, pushing aside Shiva and Narayana as if she were parting two waves in a sea, gently but firmly, and ran, fleet as the wind, towards the enemy. Her bare feet pounded the land, setting it trembling with the sound of a thousand kettle drums being struck, and a warble of a war cry emitted from her throat, high-pitched and keen.

Then her lion matched her with his own roar, stampeding the ground as he reached her side. She leapt onto his back, and they moved forward in unison. With every step, her sword slashed this way and that, cutting the demons down to the ground without a drop of sweat. Narayana and Shiva fought behind her but could not match her ferocious pace. The more she slayed, the more her bloodthirst increased. The surfeit of energies roiling through her from the time of the ceremony reached a fevered pitch.

Her feet sank into mud moistened by blood and entrails as the ranks of the rakshasas collapsed. She marched through the world, killing without mercy the tyrants and oppressors; the ones who were saved knelt on the bloodied ground in welcome and gratitude, with folded hands, calling out to her as Ma, the mother. Their devotion moved her more than anything else and renewed her intent to rid the world of that which caused their suffering. She fought on and on and on. After she covered one world, she leapt into the next, Shiva and Narayana trailing behind her. Her lion growled and snapped its jaws at anyone who tried to attack her.

After what felt like hours, or it could have been years, Narayana murmured behind her, 'Devi, you must stop. The cosmic order will break if you persist. The slaughter must stop. There has to be balance. Even some suffering, some wickedness in the world is needed.'

But the churning within her was so frenetic, she could not contain herself. Corpses of demons piled into heaps before her. A garland of skulls wove itself around her neck, but the cold sensation of bone against her skin could not still the fever within her. She could not keep herself from moving, disappearing from one corner of the sky and appearing in another. She flashed in different forms. Sometimes as this dark, skull-garlanded, wild-haired, bare-chested devi, sometimes as a girl child, sometimes as the cosmic mother whose body was comprised of all the *lokas*, sometimes as a self-decapitated devi, sometimes as the widow of death, accompanied by a crow. The fiercer she became, the louder the mortals' calls of 'Ma, Ma, Ma' rang.

It was too much. She could not bear the shakti raging within her. Somehow, she had become Shakti itself, with no limitation, no permanent form. Restlessness overtook her, and she ran hither and thither, longing for reprieve. Shiva came before her as her breath turned ragged from the torrents of energy tearing through her.

He looked like blue ice, like a vast glacier. He radiated cool, icy calm, a balm against the fire raging within her.

'Sati,' he said softly, 'you have to control yourself. The worlds will all come to ruin if you persist like this.'

He reached out to her. For a moment, his hands moved down her back in a caress, rippling like a cold blue sea against the parched fiery shore of her flesh. He was as clean and fluid as water, the line of his jaw chiselled straight, the sparkling clarity and depth of his eyes gentle and warm despite the iciness of his grip. *I could drown in him*, she thought, when she was capable of thought. She started trembling. With each shiver, volcanoes erupted and the land began quaking beneath their feet. Shiva drew her close. She could smell the fragrance of sandalwood and crushed flowers from his ash-smeared skin. It made her want to burrow into him. How had she ever found him frightening or terrible? He surrounded her. He was a refuge from everything, from herself.

As she began recovering her senses, the acrid smell of blood and gore seared her nostrils. She heard mountains crumbling behind her, she heard the screams of those she had maimed, the kin of those she had killed wailing into the skies. She turned her head to witness the destruction she had wrought, ashamed but also craving more.

Shiva cupped her head. 'Don't look, Sati. You are not ready to see it. Just look at me.'

She cringed as she felt the blood drip off the backs of her fingers, the grooves left behind on her flesh from her tight grip on her sword and bow.

She began swaying in shock. 'What have I done?

'Hush, Sati,' Shiva urged. He held the sides of her face, shielding her eyes within the fragrant, tender wall of his hands, shielding her from herself.

She could not help the whimper that left her trembling lips. Shiva sighed, muttering curses under his breath, then pulled her head to his chest gingerly, patting her shoulder awkwardly.

Narayana approached, surveying them with curiosity. He addressed Shiva. 'We'd better go back.'

Shiva nodded, and in a flash, the three of them and Sati's lion were back in the assembly hall at Mount Meru. Everything was as they had left it. What had felt like long hours in the mortal world below had passed in a thrice here. Everyone was waiting in the same seated position, now gaping at them.

Daksha jumped up in alarm and fury. 'Who are you?' He shook his staff at her. 'And what have you done with my daughter? Rakshasi! Demoness! Bring back Sati immediately!' His teeth were bared in a snarl. Before he could move towards them, Shiva threw a quelling glance in his direction. It propelled Daksha all the way to the back of the assembly hall, where he collapsed in an ungraceful heap.

Sati rushed to him. 'Father! It's me, Sati. Why are you looking at me like that?'

He covered his eyes and began mewling gibberish. 'No! No, it cannot be.'

Narayana intervened. 'Calm yourself. She is fine. Shiva and I would not have returned without her safely in our care.'

Daksha lifted a shaking finger, pointing it at her incredulously. 'Sati? How can that be my Sati? You have seen my daughter, how beautiful she is. How could this— this monstrous thing be my daughter?'

Shiva's breath hissed in warning as his eyes began flinting with angry fire. Narayana restrained him with a hand as Sati's heart began racing. She conjured a mirror into her hand and gasped at the sight of her body. A tattered deerskin skirt had replaced her red silken dress.

She was now bare-chested with a garland of skulls as a
necklace, shorn of all her precious gold ornaments. Her
skin had darkened to deep, inky black, broken by the
crimson slash of an elongated tongue that lolled out her
mouth slightly, plump with mischief and bloodthirst. Her
elegantly coiffed hair had become unbound, falling in a
mass of black curls down to the backs of her knees.

Part of her was embarrassed, but another, deeper part
secretly revelled in this version of herself. She turned
back to face the assembly hall. Her father stared at her
in disgust and horror. Her mother looked at her in
desperate worry. Saraswati and Lakshmi rushed to her
side protectively. Narayana remained close by, calm and
unmoved. Finally, her eyes moved to Shiva. She caught
him unawares before he could conceal the heat in
his eyes, an unmistakable flicker of desire. Her cheeks
flushed. Had she been just Sati, she would have shied
away from his stare. But she was more than Sati now, she
was this dark devi, too, this glowing black embodiment
of sheer power and force. She held his gaze unabashedly
until finally he looked away with a small shake of his
head.

One of the *purohits* standing next to Daksha cleared
his throat anxiously. 'Should we resume the ceremony?'
With a vague wave of his hand, he indicated all the pretty
animals patiently waiting to be chosen as Sati's *vahana*.

At her glance, they all bowed their heads, and she
smiled at them fondly. With a growl, her lion stalked over
to her side, pressing against her thigh until she ruffled his
mane.

Narayana remarked dryly, 'I believe the *vahana* has
already been chosen.'

Daksha howled in protest. 'Stop it! Stop at once. Nothing has been chosen. The ceremony has been defiled. Sati is—she must be sick, something has poisoned her. We will reconvene another time. We will start over.' He scrambled to his feet and walked towards Sati. 'Come, Sati. We will get the best vaidyas to examine you and find out what is wrong with you.'

He reached out to touch her. The lion growled. Shiva growled, too. 'Do not touch her,' he warned in a low voice. Daksha whipped his head towards Shiva in outrage. 'How dare you interfere between me and my daughter! Yama knows you must be to blame for this somehow. What did you do to her? Where did you take her when you disappeared? Your favourite cremation ground? This is too much now. She has chosen a lion? A lion? What kind of *vahana* is that? Why not the eagle or an owl or a swan? It is not...seemly. She deserves something more elegant and refined.'

Shiva's eyes narrowed in displeasure, but he maintained a calm voice as he explained, 'She is burning with too much energy, forces you cannot even fathom. If you touch her, it will be excruciating for her and deadly for you. No one and nothing in this universe can withstand her touch at this moment.'

But you did, Sati remembered. He had held her and cooled her, taken her into himself for a moment. She became wistful for that moment when everything else had ceased to exist.

The weight of what she had been through since the day had begun made her knees buckle, and she leaned into the lion for support. He immediately carried her away from the assembly hall. She melted into his warm fur in gratitude and relief. He was swift-footed and in a moment, they were at the entrance to the assembly hall, Shiva, Narayana, Lakshmi and Saraswati by their side.

'Home,' Sati whispered to her *vahana*. 'Let's go home.'

CHAPTER 7

Sati was half-conscious as her lion ferried her through starry skies to a land far away. The others followed—Narayana on Garuda, Saraswati on the wings of a snowy white swan, Lakshmi on the back of a brown owl and Shiva on Nandi. They brought her to the island of Manidvipa, Sati's abode. They flew across the Sudha Samudra, the Ocean of Nectar, crossing moats of jewel-toned water and ornate gardens to the centre of a lotus-shaped palace.

Manidvipa had been there from time immemorial, since before Sati was even born. But it belonged to her as she belonged to it. It was her place of strength and succour, where she retreated when she wanted to be on her own. It was a manifestation of her essence. Four halls comprising one thousand pillars grew successively larger, leading to her inner chamber. On top of each hall were strewn canopies of various colours scented by incense and musk. A nearby pond was brimming with lotuses and blanketed with bees. Swans drifted to and fro. On all sides were flowing rivers of ghee, milk, yoghurt, honey, nectar, pomegranate and sugarcane juice.

Mere mortals were not allowed here. In fact, no one was allowed here but Sati herself. Even her father had to beg permission for entrance. It was only at her sleepy nod that the celestial guardians standing at the door to her chamber allowed the others in.

Shiva picked her up and placed her on the bed. She fell into a deep, dreamless sleep.

Many hours later, she woke to the murmur of voices around her. 'Should we wake her?' asked Saraswati anxiously. 'She does not look well at all. She's not back to our Sati yet. We must summon Dhanvantari here to care for her. I do not know what sickness this is.'

Shiva interrupted sharply, 'She is not sick. There is nothing wrong with her.'

Saraswati's voice quickened in anger. 'She is suffering! Even in her sleep, she has been moaning in pain. Look at her skin, it is bruising blue and black from within. She has goosebumps all over. It's as if she is rejecting whatever this form is, this blackness of Kali.'

Shiva waved a dismissive hand. 'She is just getting used to it. How boring would it be to be the same form all the time? Finally, she is becoming a little interesting! Don't ruin it now.'

I must be feeling better, thought Sati, remembering the heat in his gaze when he had looked at her as Kali. *I'm able to blush again.*

The ever-perceptive Narayana said, 'I do believe she is awake.'

The others fell silent as Sati opened her eyes. She lifted her arm to her face and observed it was still the same black hue as earlier, fading slightly into indigo. She peeked down and was relieved to see she was at least now covered by a blanket, her chest no longer bare. She offered a wan smile of reassurance to her sisters. In a moment, her lion bounded to her side from the other corner of the chamber, snarling softly as he sniffed and inspected her. She patted his head affectionately.

Lakshmi sat next to her, keeping her distance from the lion. 'He has not left your side since we got here,' she said. 'By the way, what are you going to call him? Now that he's your *vahana*?'

'Dawon,' she replied promptly.

'Hmm... Interesting name.'

She could not resist looking towards Shiva. Narayana was standing next to him, observing them both with keen interest.

Shiva opened and closed his mouth a few times, as if he was about to say something, then abruptly announced, 'I'll be on my way then. You will be fine now.'

Sati sputtered, 'You can't leave!'

Shiva raised his arms with his palms turned upwards. 'Why not? You are in good hands here. Your sisters know how to look after you. You just need some time and rest. As I said, you will be just fine.' He said it with the blasé confidence of one who wove the fabric of the cosmos, whose word was the will of the universe.

'What will happen to me?' she whispered. It terrified her, how she had spontaneously changed form what felt like millions of times, how she had killed gluttonously, how she could have destroyed entire worlds.

Shiva shooed away Lakshmi and sat next to her. He was impersonal now, an ancient deva, who was present before the first emanation of the universe, from before the first turning of the wheel of the first Manvantara, looking at her as if she was so very young.

'Nothing happened,' he said. At moments, it was as if fire smouldered within him, held back by that thin layer of ash smeared on his body. 'All that happened is that you saw a glimmer, just a glimmer, of what you are. You are not just Sati. You are Shakti.' At her frown, he smiled softly. 'You do not understand what that means...yet. No matter. One day, you will. I hope.' His smile turned wistful and faraway, as if he was remembering something from long ago.

'Will I stay like this, as Kali?'

He tilted his head contemplatively. 'It will wear off. Your base form is that of Sati. You can and will become Kali, Durga, so many other names and forms, as you desire and as is needed for the protection of dharma. This is the first time it has happened, so you will take a little longer to come back to your usual self. Nothing to worry about.'

He did not wait for an answer. He simply turned around and walked out, Narayana running to catch up with him.

♋

'She is stronger than we are,' said Narayana admiringly. They were at the outskirts of Manidvipa, on the edge of the inky black starry skies that separated the planets. Garuda and Nandi were napping before their long journeys home. Narayana would retire to Ksheera Sagara to rest and meditate while Lakshmi looked after Sati. Shiva was on his way back to Kailash.

Shiva laughed. 'Of course, she is. She is Shakti, the very force of life and creation itself. What can be stronger than her?'

Narayana leaned back against Garuda's folded wings, crossing his arms. He remarked, 'Indeed, you seemed quite enamoured with her.'

Shiva sniffed. 'You have been spending too much time meddling in the lives of mortals. Do not try those tricks with me.'

Now Narayana leaned forward. 'But imagine how much fun it would be, how many rakshasas we can slay with her at our side. It doesn't have to be just the two of us any more. Other than worrying she was going to destroy the universe, it was really enjoyable, the three of us side by side, defeating the forces of wickedness.'

Shiva stiffened. He drew out his chillum and lit it. 'Do not be so lazy that you make her take undue risk, Narayana. She is only to come out when we need her and have no other choice.'

Narayana smiled. 'Don't worry. We will never let her come to harm.'

Shiva said nothing.

'Tell me you do not find her beautiful.'

'Of course, she is beautiful,' Shiva replied neutrally. 'She is the most magnificent of the devis. She has to, by nature, be beautiful. If I have eyes, of course, they will behold beauty. That is only logical. But it does not mean anything. She has her work. We have ours. When we are to work together, of course, we will. That is the wheel of dharma. Nothing more.'

Narayana's smile widened. 'But have you ever found anyone beautiful before?'

Shiva tilted his head, considering. He sorted through millions of years' worth of memories, which took a few chuffs of his chillum to contemplate. So many apsaras, so many devis, none of whom had caught his eye.

'No, I suppose not,' he conceded. Before Narayana could speak any further, Shiva broke in, 'Do not try to domesticate me, Narayana. It is my *tapasya* that sustains the order of the cosmos, that keeps the suns and stars burning and the planets orbiting on their axes. The entire purpose of my manifestation is to burn myself in penance and destroy when destruction is warranted, to keep the cycles of the ages going through my dance of death. I am not you. I am all that is horrid in the worlds, I am friend to the ghosts, goblins and the forsaken. I while away the days and nights by cremation pyres when I am not in the glaciers and jungles, in places too dreadful for any other living creature, let alone one like Sati. Do not speak to me of beauty or love. That is not for me.'

As Garuda awoke, fluttering his wings, Narayana sat astride him. 'I have a good memory, too, Shiva. You and I have the same memories. We are not subject to time or maya, the power of cosmic delusion that renders all mortals ignorant of the underlying reality of oneness. You know as well as I do that in all cycles past and to come, in all permutations of the creation and destruction of the universe, she has always been with you. When she comes into her own, she, too, will know this. Why then resist?'

Shiva took one last puff of the chillum before patting Nandi on his rump to stir him from sleep. 'Is it always the same, you think? The cycles of time, do they always repeat this way? Do we not have a choice? By whose will am I the Destroyer and you the Preserver of life? Who can dare challenge our will if we were to want things a different way? Are we devas just puppets of fate? If not, then why do you assume it will be the same way this time just because it has been that one way all times past?'

Narayana replied impatiently. 'You have been spending too much time with the rishis, who are always asking these kinds of questions. There is no purpose seeking reason or logic when there is none. It is *leela*, the cosmic play, that is all. No cause is required for that which is causeless, that which just is.'

Shiva said flatly, 'My *leela* right now is to enjoy a most wondrous solitude in Kailash. See you when I see you, Narayana.' And with an affectionate wave, he took off on Nandi's back in one direction while Narayana and Garuda set out in another.

CHAPTER 8

Never before in her life had Sati moped. Yet now, even as she healed and recovered, reverting to her natural form, she could not shake off the melancholy that had settled into her belly. It pricked her awake from restless dreams, dulled her taste buds and dimmed the lustre of the red and pink blossoms that lined her daily walks through Mount Meru upon her return from Manidvipa. Weeks passed but her sadness did not dissipate.

Lakshmi and Saraswati did their best to cheer her up, assuming that she was traumatised from the events of the *vahana* ceremony. But that was not it at all. She was bereft. She was haunted by tawny matted locks, gleaming reddened eyes that smouldered from within, long, tapering fingers gliding like smooth icicles across her skin. It was such a blur, the happenings of that day, no more than a hazy dream. Had she imagined this connection with Shiva? Was it all in her head?

Lakshmi and Saraswati were arguing about how best to make Sati feel better. Saraswati still wanted to bring in Dhanvantari to examine her.

Lakshmi scoffed. 'What do you need a doctor for? It's obvious she is lovesick.'

Sati blushed beet-red.

Saraswati was nonplussed. She wrinkled her brows. 'Lovesick? For whom?'

The way Saraswati's wide eyes tilted upward and to the left for long moments, Sati could tell she was scanning her encyclopaedic memory through the pantheon of the devas to figure out whom Sati could possibly be attracted to. Sati's stomach sank in dread, imagining Saraswati's reaction when she would discover the truth about her feelings for Shiva.

Anyway, what was the point of her learning the truth? There had been no word from Shiva, so even if she had not imagined the flicker of interest on his end, it had apparently fizzled away to nothing.

Lakshmi, either oblivious to or deliberately ignoring Sati's imploring gaze, remarked brightly, 'Shiva, who else?'

Saraswati's face turned from ivory to ashen, and her rosebud mouth dropped open. 'Shiva? No, it cannot possibly be!' But when her piercing eyes turned to Sati's flushed face, she realised it was actually so. With a swish of her red-bordered white satin sari, Saraswati sat next to Sati, tenderly grasping her shoulders as if to shake the infatuation out of her.

'Sati, please think clearly.' Saraswati was wisdom personified and expected everyone to be as logical and clear-thinking as she was. 'I know he is...magnetic and powerful, but he is not suitable for marriage. The only company he keeps is that of those horrifying *ganas*. He has never had a family. He is not the marrying kind. He wouldn't even know how to treat you. He can barely get through the brief days he spends on Mount Meru without breaking apart the mountain and all those who live here or going mad with boredom himself.'

Sati looked down, twisting her wrists on her lap. None of this could she deny. Saraswati was relentless. 'Even if he was willing to marry you, what would your life together be? Roaming together in cremation grounds? Wasting away on some remote glacier in the freezing cold? That's hardly the life for you.'

'No, that's not what I want,' Sati acknowledged in a mumble.

Saraswati folded her arms across her chest and tapped her right arm with the fingers of her left hand impatiently. 'Then, what do you want?'

Sati lifted her head. 'I want him,' she said plainly.

She got up and began pacing the hexagonal chamber in which they were drinking mint-infused lavender tea. The entire room was bathed in pastels—blush-coloured woven tapestries and pink marbled walls. They were high up in a tower in the palace they shared. From here she could see the splendour of Mount Meru spread at her feet—the red stone of the steep mountain with twisting, winding gem-paved walkways carpeted by rolling, verdant forests speckled with the rarest, most beautiful birds nestling among the highest branches.

Sati marvelled at the sight of her home even as she was deep in reflection. She could not explain her attraction to Shiva. It was elemental, as necessary and intrinsic to her being as breath itself. It was not something she could analyse. Simply thinking of his name, breathing in those two syllables, was enough to suffuse her with such warmth, light and strength that she needed nothing else.

Saraswati joined her at the window, putting an arm around her shoulders with a loving squeeze. She pressed her lips into her hair. 'You've grown up, sister. You're coming into your own. It is indeed time for you to marry, as your father has been saying. Just not Shiva, dear. Anyone but him.'

Sati stiffened and stepped back, and Saraswati sighed as both her sisters glared at her angrily.

Saraswati murmured to herself, 'One day, you will see I am right.'

♋

'It's too bad that Narayana is already taken,' said Daksha Prajapati. 'He would have been the ideal husband for my beloved Sati.'

Sati rolled her eyes. 'Oh, Pitashree, honestly!'

'It is true! The most elegant and refined of the devas with the most beautiful and elegant of devis!'

'Lakshmi is the most beautiful, elegant and refined of all of us!' protested Sati hotly on behalf of her sister.

Maharishi Bhrigu cleared his throat. He was a knower of the stars, one of the Saptarishis, the great seven sages. He studied the patterns of the stars and used them to divine the past, present and future, spurring the creation of a whole new field known as *jyotisha*, Vedic astrology. This had proven more popular than expected with the mortals, and so he was preoccupied much of the time in drawing up charts and predictions to satisfy the curiosity of both immortals, including gandharvas and apsaras, and mortals.

Daksha had summoned him in desperation. The *vahana* ceremony had appalled him. He was convinced Sati was at risk of self-destruction if she was not put on the proper path, and who better to guide her than a husband carefully handpicked by her loving father? So Daksha had redoubled his efforts to find her a suitable match.

Bhrigu himself was baffled to have been summoned. As much as he enjoyed visiting Mount Meru to meet with the devas and have the most illuminating discussions and debates with the other rishis, he was never called to consult. The stars controlled the fates of the mortals, but how could those who controlled the stars themselves be subject to the whims and fancies of their patterns and forces?

Daksha dismissed his objections. 'No, no, revered Maharishi. I have not asked you to come here to make predictions. That choice is up to m—to us,' he corrected hastily with a patronising glance at his daughter. 'But you see the patterns in the universe, the forces at play. You have studied so many thousands and millions of lives and know what brings happiness, what brings sorrow, which matches are auspicious and which are dangerous. From that perspective, please tell us what you think about Sati's impending marriage.'

Bhrigu shook his head. 'You are overthinking things, Daksha. As you mentioned Narayana and his most auspicious marriage with Lakshmi, just remember how naturally and easily did that occur! No sooner had she emerged from the churning of the waters than her eyes fell upon Narayana. All the devas who stood there desired her. She was the most beautiful female anyone had ever seen. But her fate and Narayana's were sealed the moment their eyes met. She did not even look at anyone else. She garlanded him, and they were married at that moment.'

'Did Shiva desire Lakshmi, too?' She uttered the words aloud without realising and Bhrigu's eyebrows shot up while her father glared at her.

Bhrigu remarked drily, 'I think he was rather preoccupied at the moment.'

Sati flushed in embarrassment. Of course. Before Lakshmi had emerged, it was the deadly toxic fumes of the most potent poison, Halahala, that had been churned out of the milky ocean. Shiva had held it in his throat.

She was reminded of what she had wanted to say to Saraswati earlier, 'It is because he does all these things we think terrible, because he stays in terrible places, because he keeps company with the terrible ones, absorbs and channels all the terrible energies, that he has the strength to take and destroy that which is most terrible; he and no one else, not even Narayana.' *And maybe*, she thought to herself, *maybe when I am Kali, I can do things that Sati could never do*. It was Shiva who had unlocked that aspect of herself and allowed her to unleash it.

Daksha harrumphed. 'Well, it would be nice if such a thing had happened to my Sati. But she is old enough now and no such miraculous meeting of the eyes has taken place. I really do not know what to do.'

Bhrigu replied in an even tone, 'There are thirty-three million devas. Surely there must be an eligible match somewhere in there.' He smirked at Sati. 'Unless there already is such a match and she is just too shy to tell us.'

Sati shook her head. Months had passed now and there was still no word from Shiva. What was the point of admitting an unrequited love? Lakshmi had urged her to write to Shiva, to send Garuda there with a message on her behalf, but Sati did not know what she could say to him. She thought of sending a gift, but what was a good gift to send to the greatest renunciate? She ended up sending a basket of hay for Nandi that she especially grew for him, cultivating a breed that would be most flavourful and texturally pleasing for a very picky, aloof bull.

Daksha said despondently, 'There is no one to equal Sati in all of Mount Meru, no one I can consider a good match for her.'

Sati threw an appealing look at her mother to stop this melodrama, but Prasuti shrugged helplessly and poured out more tea, arranging the snacks, even though Bhrigu did not drink tea and ate only fruit.

Bhrigu replied, 'It is not always good for like to marry like. Many of the best pairings are between opposites.'

Sati looked at him with new interest. 'Oh, do say more, please, Maharishi.'

'The best couples are greater together than the sum of their individual parts. Their natures should be complementary and harmonious rather than too similar. There is a reason why opposites attract.'

Daksha was growing impatient. 'This is too much theory. Too abstract. Get to the specifics now, please, Maharishi. I know how learned you are. You study the stars and the movements of the planets. You study the forces that shape our universe. Surely you must be able to see something about the future of the best of my daughters.'

The air thickened and grew heavy with tension. Bhrigu loomed larger, a vortex of vibrating energy gathering around him. His voice grew deep and sombre. Politesse dropped. His eyes narrowed and pierced Daksha. 'There are greater forces than what you describe, forces so subtle and foundational that they are beyond my or any mortal's study or even perception. There are matters from which the tongue and mind curl back, which even the Saptarishis are unqualified to speak about. You are asking questions I cannot answer. Your daughter is beyond my study, beyond my gaze. I can only bow before her. Do not ask me for what I cannot say.'

Daksha fell to his knees. 'Please. I do not know what is happening to her. I feel... I have felt for some time now that the key is to arrange a good marriage for her. I cannot explain it, but I know in my bones that it is of utmost importance that she has the right husband.'

'On that, you are correct,' Bhrigu said softly.

'Please. I am a worried father. Tell me whatever you can. Tell me what you see.'

Bhrigu turned to Sati, seeking her permission. She nodded. She was anxious, too.

He closed his eyes and withdrew his senses, retreating into himself. Long minutes passed before he spoke. The skies outside darkened and the air chilled as if Bhrigu pulled all light and warmth into himself to divine the future. Finally, as Sati started shivering, he spoke.

'I see two paths. On one there is contentment and stability. There is harmony and security. It is untroubled and peaceful. The other...the other is the path of her heart. I see... I see turmoil and conflict. A golden discus and a raging fire. I see destruction...and death. A tragic death. I see the sun and stars, the planets, whirling off their axes into a vortex of endless destruction and darkness.' He shook and suddenly awoke as if whatever he saw was too awful to contemplate.

Daksha's face was ashen. 'We need to get on the first path. Who is that husband? Who is the one who can give her peace and stability, security and harmony? Who can give her happiness?'

Bhrigu's eyes darkened, troubled. He replied flatly, 'Such a one does not exist.'

♋

Sati twirled a strand of glossy black hair around her thumb as she inhaled the fragrance of the sweet strawberry tea that Lakshmi had prepared for her.

'Maybe I am destined to never be married,' she said dreamily. 'Like a warrior queen who is wed only to her work of ridding the world of demons and darkness. Alone and aloof, fit only to be worshipped but not loved.'

Saraswati scoffed, 'Even when contemplating a life alone, sister, you are such a romantic. I know even right now, you are thinking of he who would break all barriers to be by your side and fight your demons for you.'

Sati's eyes dropped to the steaming pink tea in her copper cup. Her sister was half-right. But the daydream was not of being rescued by him, but of fighting alongside him, living and working with him, like two halves of a whole. And it was not some faceless hero. It was, of course, Shiva. He had captured her waking moments and now even her dreams.

Lakshmi sat next to her on the cushioned floor, patting her hand comfortingly. 'Sati, you are the greatest of the devis. Everybody knows this. Your destiny will not be decided by the fate of the stars when even the moon is nothing more than an adornment for your hair. Neither your father nor the greatest of the devas is going to command you to do this or that. If you want to marry, of course, you will be married. If the one who deserves you has not yet been born, we will turn the wheels of fate so that he is born immediately. Sati, as soon as you know what you want, you shall have it!'

Saraswati said softly, 'Oh, she knows. She just does not want to admit it.'

Sati's face flamed, and she looked away from both her sisters. What was the point of admitting she wanted Shiva when he gave no indication of wanting her? Not to mention the disturbance it would cause in Devaloka. Her father would not accept it. He would tear up the heavens with his fury. Everyone would be scandalised. Shiva was the one who had saved the universe, but everyone feared him, his extremes, his terribleness, the brutal strength and power by which he could contain in his throat the poisons of the world.

Before she could reply, Daksha walked into the chamber with an abrupt knock on the door. A sheen of sweat shone on his jowled face. 'Daughter, I must talk to you.' His voice was breathless, as anxious as Sati had ever seen him.

She hurried to his side. 'What's wrong, Pitashree?' She sat him down on a chair.

He gripped her hands. 'Daughter, I do not care what Maharishi Bhrigu or anybody else says. I will not let any harm or unhappiness touch you. I've been thinking about this night and day, how to solve our problem. I have found one solution and have come here to tell you about it.'

Sati cast a look at her sisters.

Daksha said, 'Let them stay. I know you will only tell them about it as soon as I leave, so they may as well hear about it straight from me.'

They settled on the floor, close to him. He closed his eyes to take a breath. 'This is not the first I have thought about your marriage, Sati. Some time ago, I had even gone to the Trimurti to talk about it—Brahma, Narayana and Shiva. At that time, I proposed some names, but Shiva rejected them all as not being worthy of you.'

Lakshmi winked at Sati.

'Well, he was not completely wrong.' Despite himself, Daksha could not keep his disdain for Shiva from his voice. 'I really do not see any suitable groom for you in Devaloka.'

Lakshmi's eyes widened. 'Must we churn the Ksheera Sagara again to bring forth a new deva for Sati, like how I came out and was immediately wed to Narayana?'

Sati's father sighed. 'There's no ocean churning currently being planned,' he deadpanned. 'But you are on the right track, Devi. I am not waiting on the ocean or fate. There is one thing more powerful than fate. It is the divine will, the will of the devas. We will combine the forces of the devas to create a new deva, an ideal husband for Sati. I have already reached out to all of the devas—well, most of them. They have agreed to do this.'

Sati's jaw dropped. 'Pitashree, that's... that's abhorrent! That's unnatural. We cannot ask such a thing, do such a thing. It must be against dharma.'

Daksha jumped to his feet and began pacing. 'Did you even hear the Maharishi, Sati? There is no one in existence who can keep you from pain and death. I will not allow your death. Never. Whatever it takes. I am the *purohit* to the devas! For so many thousands of years, I have presided over countless yajnas to ensure the well-being and harmony of all life in all the worlds. Never have I asked anything for myself. But this one time I insist. This time, they dare not defy me!'

His words were so vehement that Sati quavered.

He continued in a thunderous voice. 'In two days, they will all gather for the sacrifice. There is no time to lose.'

Sati wondered if he had reached out to Shiva, and how he would have responded. Her throat turned dry. *What if he has agreed?*

'So, the Trimurti agreed?' She tried to sound as neutral as possible.

Daksha grunted. 'Brahma and Narayana have, of course. I would not dare to do anything without their permission. I am not bothering to inform Shiva. He is not needed for this.'

Saraswati warned, 'You should be careful of leaving him out of the yajnas. You cannot cavalierly ignore him. It is a great insult, and he is Mahadeva after all.'

Daksha merely grunted again. His short arms punched the air. 'He has never cared about weddings or such affairs. I am sure he will not mind.'

Lakshmi interjected, 'Oh, but he will definitely care about Sati's marriage.' Sati threw her a murderous look to shut her up.

Daksha was so intent on his own thoughts, though, that he did not notice.

He opened the door to leave as abruptly as he had entered. 'I must go make all the preparations. Of course, nothing like this has ever been attempted before, so I am bringing together all the *purohits* and other knowledgeable ones to plan this properly. Be ready, daughter, two days from now.' And he closed the door firmly behind him.

CHAPTER 9

Sati ushered her sisters out after her father had left. She wanted to be alone. By the time she left home for a walk, it was late at night. She told herself she had no destination in mind, but she ended up at the cottage at the end of the lane at the edge of Mount Meru where Shiva had stayed before the Night of Rudra, which had now been renamed Shivaratri, the Night of Shiva.

It was forlorn now. The tree where the white flowers had bloomed was nothing more than a dried-up fossil, its branches swaying morosely in the wind. There was a coldness here as if the air were bereft without Shiva.

'I know how you feel,' whispered Sati. She felt bereft without him, too. Being here, where he had once been, made her miss him even more.

Tears pricked her eyes. Before they could fall, a voice said stiffly behind her, 'You are not allowed to cry.'

Sati stifled a gasp as her heartbeat quickened. She tried to compose her face, to smooth it of all emotion, before she turned around to face Shiva. He loomed large in the shadows, radiant as ash against the charcoal night sky. Nandi was next to him, his nose sniffing the air inquisitively.

'What are you doing here?'

His wide, muscled shoulders shrugged. 'There seemed to be some kind of ruckus going on around here, and I wanted to make sure there was nothing wrong.' Nandi tilted his head sceptically at Shiva as if challenging the truth of his words.

Her hands fidgeted and knotted the end of her sari as she explained, 'It's my father. He's...arranging a ceremony in two days, so things are very hectic.'

He stalked towards her until he was mere inches away. His eyes were fathomless. Nandi poked his head in the grass, grazing contentedly.

'Why were you about to cry?'

Her eyes fell away from his gaze. 'The ceremony is related to my marriage. My father wants to create a groom for me by gathering together the energies of all the devas...well, most of the devas.' It was mortifying telling him about this.

Nandi's snort of laughter was muffled by the grass in which he was grazing. Shiva's eyes focused on her face.

'And you have agreed to this?'

'N-no, not exactly.' She hated the wishy-washy tone of her voice.

A muscle in his jaw tightened, as if he was annoyed, too. 'I do not like being here. It is crowded. I do not want to see anyone and deal with their nonsense. It is time I leave.'

He gestured with his index finger to Nandi, who immediately trotted to his side. He gave her a curt nod and turned away.

Her eyes filled with tears.

Shiva grunted, still turned away. 'Not again. Stop that now.'

'How can you even tell I'm about to cry? I didn't even make a sound. How is it you are so oblivious to everyone and everything in this place, and yet you get disturbed by something as trivial as my tears?'

'How is it that you cry so much?' Annoyance sharpened his voice.

This was it. If he left now, she would never meet him again. She was certain of it. The last time he had seen her, she had been Kali. She had been bold and brave then, not shy of anything. She was tired of being shy.

'If you don't want me to cry, then don't leave.' She said the words firmly and clearly.

He took a lightning-quick stride to her side, his eyes suddenly warm. He held her by the elbow. 'Come with me. Let us talk, but not here.'

He helped her onto Nandi's back and sat behind her.

'Where are we going?'

'Home,' he whispered into her ear, and they took off into the starry sky.

♋

Sati felt warm and safe tucked against Shiva's chest as they rushed as fast as the wind through vast expanses of sky, sea and land. When she travelled, she liked to float and drift. But Shiva, as he rode Nandi, was fast and rough. Nandi's hooves pounded the surfaces of moons, his legs scissored as they swam through seas, slid softly through the sands of endless deserts. The wind ripped through their hair, the salt of the oceans stung their skin, the suns of distant worlds warmed their cheeks.

Sati was exhausted by the time Nandi's gait slowed to a saunter. They had entered a territory of endless ice and snow. It felt as if they were in the furthest reaches of the universe. The temperature dropped steeply. She yawned and shivered against Shiva's chest. He breathed out slowly and his body warmed beneath her body, driving away the cold.

She lifted her head to see the world around her. *This must be Kailash*, she thought. It was a snowy wilderness. They were in the midst of a ring of jagged icy mountain peaks that stood like daggers, fiercely protecting the realm within. Looking back, Sati could not detect where Nandi had entered. It seemed as if there was no way in, no way out.

There was a faint ringing in her ears from the total soundlessness of the world. There was no motion in the air, not even the ripple of a breeze. There was no vegetation here, no insects, nothing other than Shiva, Nandi and, in the distance, what appeared to be hordes of *ganas*, all on the lookout for their master. Shiva dismounted from Nandi with Sati still in his arms. He sent Nandi off to rest with an affectionate thump on his rump. Sati wondered what Nandi could possibly eat here. She wished she had brought him some grass to chew on from Mount Meru. She slid down from Shiva's arms, her feet momentarily unsteady on the slippery ice. He held her upright, his hand warm on her lower back.

With his touch, they zoomed across the ice, reaching the base of the mountain that appeared to be his residence.

The *ganas* stared at them, openly gossiping with one another. 'Who is this strange woman? Why is she here?

She's not one of us. What is Shiva doing? Has there ever been a woman in our world?' They did not bother to keep their voices down or avert their gazes as she offered them weak smiles.

In truth, at that moment, she was a little frightened. Some of them were giants, towering over two tree heights. Some had horns on their heads. Some had multiple heads. Some looked like vicious killers. Some were accomplished robbers she had personally seen chased out of Mount Meru.

Shiva was impervious to their words and stares, nodding at them absent-mindedly as he drew her through their midst to the edge of the wall of the mountain. All thoughts of the *ganas* receded from her mind as the magnificent mountain filled her with awe. She did not think even she could scale it. What moons, what worlds, what constellations had she not conquered with her feet, yet the imposing steep height of this peak left her breathless. It was slicked with ice, sheer and devoid of any pocks in the grey-black hard stone that could serve as footholds. Even ants would fall off its side if they attempted to climb it.

Her throat turned dry.

She had pondered what it was like at the top of Kailash, where Shiva resided. She knew he would not have a palace like the other devas. But did he have any shelter at all? Was there even a cave to cover his head? Or did he live on top of the snows, bare to the elements even in sleep? Did he even sleep? If she were to live here with him, would she live like that, too?

She cleared her throat.

'If you are uncomfortable, I can take you back to your home in an instant.' His voice was cool but kind. His eyes were more inscrutable than the mysteries of the universe. There was a subtle challenge in the tilt of his tawny eyebrows.

Sati cleared her throat once more. 'No, of course not. Your home is very...lovely.'

Shiva threw his head back and laughed. The *ganas* guffawed and hooted with laughter as if she had said the most ridiculous thing. The embarrassment in her flushed face sobered him, and with a flick of his hand, Shiva dismissed the *ganas* and they scattered away.

When it was just the two of them, Shiva leaned against the mountain. He puffed from his chillum.

'Your father did not ask me, but Brahma did. I will never agree to participate in such a ceremony.'

'Because you do not want me to be married to anyone else?' she asked hopefully.

He snorted. 'No, because my energies are incompatible with anyone else's. They would destroy all the other devas' energies. It would never work. It is impossible.'

'Then you would have created another Shiva to marry this Sati,' she teased.

Shiva's eyes lit up. 'That's an idea. One Shiva to sit in isolation and meditation. The other to be your husband.'

Sati brushed particles of stray snow from her dress, her fingers fast and furious. 'You can stay one Shiva in isolation and meditation. There is no need for you to marry me. I will be quite all right by myself. You do not have to concern yourself with my marriage at all.'

She turned away from him, her back stiff. 'Now, if you do not mind giving me the directions back home, I will leave.'

Shiva clasped her shoulders and turned her around slowly. 'Were you hoping I would be jealous? Or possessive? I've heard about such things among the mortals. I never thought anyone would try it with me. I am beyond such things, my dear.'

Sati bristled. 'I was hoping for no such thing. You were the one who interrupted my walk, not the other way around. Please spare me your accusations.'

'Of course, I am not opposed to marrying you.'

Sati glared at him. 'Why would you not be opposed, if you are beyond all these things?' Petulance roughened her voice. She turned away from him, determined to go back to Mount Meru.

'Sati.' His voice was a whisper.

She tightened her shoulders in resolution. Each step away from him left her bared to the frigid cold of the snows and glacier. She already missed his warmth. If she called out to Dawon, would he be able to come here and take her home?

Shiva approached her, close enough that when he spoke his breath ruffled the small tendrils of hair curling over her ear. 'Look at this place, Sati. How can I ask you to call this place home?'

She took in the unending white of the snowy land, the grey of the stormy skies, the thin air that made her eyes smart. It was not a world she would have created. Yet, she did not want to leave. His presence surrounded her, filled her, enlivened her.

She closed her eyes. This time, he did not touch her. A hum started in her ear, like a bee murmuring. One by one, the elements vanished. The sky evaporated. The snow-laden ground fell away from her feet. The mountains obliterated. Nandi and the *ganas* disappeared. Only Shiva remained.

Earlier, the nothingness had frightened her. But now she knew it was not nothing. Even when form disappeared, even when the universe dropped away, something remained. He and she, intertwined into one. He was the inhale, she the exhale. She was the sinuous unfurling of fire, of heat and light and kinetic energy, drawn forth from the depths of formless existence within him. They melded together, fire and ice, male and female, the stillness and the whirlwind, harshness and beauty. He grounded her, and she manifested him.

When it became too intense, Sati opened her eyes and spun around to face Shiva. His eyes were half-lidded, his expression a little drunken. He held his hand out to her. Only when his fingers wrapped around her palm did she realise she had gone white with cold. He drew her to him and rubbed warmth into her skin, soothing her trembles with tiny caresses across the backs of her shoulders and arms.

She rested her cheek against his bare chest. His breath was ragged, and Sati was pleased to know she was not the only one affected.

'I think you are my home,' she said, this time her voice firm.

He tightened his arms around her until she could no longer breathe. 'Let us get married, Sati. Right away.' The rough urgency in his voice delighted Sati no end.

It was late by the time Shiva and Sati returned to Mount Meru on Nandi's back. They had lost all sense of time in their embrace, and more than a whole day had passed. Darkness had fallen, a heavy twilight of grey-black. The glistening of the white snow against the shadows of evening created a mesmerising sight. Nandi's pace was slower on the way back, expressing their unanimous reluctance to return to the world of the devas. Silence greeted them as they disembarked at the centre of the mountain, close to the assembly hall. Sati was dismayed to realise that all the devas had already gathered inside for the ceremony to create her husband.

She saw her father pacing outside, looking this way and that, searching desperately for her. She ran up to him.

'Pitashree! Pitashree! I am here.'

Daksha was relieved. His hands trembled as he clasped her shoulders tightly. His entire face lit up as he looked at her happily.

'Oh, daughter! You are here. I was so worried. Sati, did I frighten you? You know all that I do is because I love you, don't you? I was so afraid that you had left forever. There were so many things I wanted to tell you, so much that I have left to share with you. I thought I might never see you again.'

Sati's eyes teared. She squeezed his hand. 'Pitashree, I am here. Nothing will ever take me away from you.'

A shadow fell between them, a foreboding of grief and destruction to come, but they both ignored it in this moment of reunion. Daksha pulled on her hand.

'Sati, come. The ceremony has already started. The auspicious hour was about to run out, so we had to begin without you. But, come, let us join them quickly before it is too late.'

'I-I cannot, Pitashree.' Her hand dropped from his.

He wheeled around. 'What do you mean? What are you saying?' All traces of softness disappeared from his face and voice.

'I cannot participate in this ceremony.'

Then, a thunderous sound emanated from the assembly hall as the cries of thousands of officiating brahmanas crescendoed together in a frenzy.

Shiva stepped forward. 'This is getting out of hand. Do you even know what you have done? The creation of a deva is not something anyone of us can do. Devas are not created; they manifest in the universe only when needed for the wheel of dharma to continue to turn. It is not up to you or me to interfere with the order of the universe and create something which was not intended to exist. If this continues, there will be great chaos and destruction.'

Daksha sputtered ineffectually as Shiva moved past him into the assembly hall. Sati and her father ran in after him. All the devas were in a deep trance, faces and hands upturned. The chanting of hymns and invocations was mellifluous and grave. The sacrificial fire was wild, the flames dancing frenetically like apsaras in abandon.

Vast columns of energies and the essences of the various devas whirled in the air above their heads, hissing and blazing as they mixed and intermingled. Some devas were convulsing from the exertion of channelling their energies into the yajna. A few had already collapsed. The *purohits* were groaning in pain, some bleeding from their noses. Above the flames, the hazy outline of a masculine form started to take shape, alarming Sati. Were they too late?

Daksha threw up his hands. 'I do not know what is happening.' His tone turned imperious as he nodded stiffly in Shiva's direction. 'I suppose you can go ahead and fix all this.'

Shiva's lip curled downward in contempt. Daksha was oblivious, simply staring at him with expectant eyes.

Shiva cleared his throat and released a long 'Om'. It came from the base of his throat, deeper than the rumbling of an earthquake. It reverberated through the assembly hall and stilled the shaking bodies of the devas. It brought the officiating brahamanas to silence. It calmed the flames of the sacrificial fire. It stilled the swirls of energies that were colliding in the air above their heads. But he could not reverse what had already been started; the energies emanating from the devas had already been released. Shiva exhaled lightly, generating a breeze that ruffled through the assembly hall and roused the devas.

They blinked open their eyes as Shiva requested, in a gentle voice so as not to agitate them any further, 'My dear devas, it is neither appropriate nor necessary to create a new deva for Sati to marry. Instead, allow me to take all of your essences combined to fashion a worthy gift for her. Shower all your energies and powers into one sword which shall always adorn her, with which she will defend all of us and the *rtam*. With this sword, may she be the protectress of us all.'

Seemingly out of nowhere, Narayana sidled up to Shiva with a bright smile on his face. As the other devas nodded in consent, Narayana asked, 'What kind of gift is this, brother? A wedding gift?' He winked conspiratorially at Sati.

Shiva bristled. 'Don't start with all that again. Why don't you sit down and participate like everyone else?' As

Narayana sat on the floor with a smirk, Shiva threw him a sidelong glance. 'I see you did not participate in the first idiotic ceremony.'

Narayana chuckled. 'Oh, I did not dare! Not if I wanted to keep my head. Between you and my wife, I'm not sure who would have decapitated me first.'

Shiva shushed him. 'Be quiet. Let me get on with this.'

Narayana's smile deepened until his blue cheeks dimpled. 'Are you not going to contribute your energies to this weapon, Shiva?'

'There is no need. I will always be with her.'

This time, Sati smiled, too.

♋

Shiva and Sati let Brahma, Daksha and the others sort out the details of the timing and logistics of the wedding. They only wanted to get married as soon as possible. Daksha was suitably chastened and would interfere no longer. Sati's mother just wished for her daughter's happiness. The devas secretly delighted in the idea of Shiva being domesticated.

The conclave to decide on the details of the wedding ceremony was held at Daksha's palace. The wedding of the greatest of the devas and the greatest of the devis was an event in which all the denizens of Mount Meru felt vested. Such an auspicious union was not only a matter of happiness for the families concerned but also a great blessing for the world.

As they sat through the long hours of poring over astrological charts, arcane tomes on rites and debates between great pandits, Sati dared not look at Shiva for fear of turning into a beet with all her blushing. She sat across the sitting room from him, deliberately ignoring him every time he looked at her with open interest and attraction.

Saraswati and Lakshmi sat on either side of her. They were the last to remain as the palace gradually emptied over the night. Finally, Sati's parents went to bed, exhausted after such a hectic day. Shiva made to leave and Lakshmi ran after him. She threw a wink at Sati. 'I must have a word with my future brother-in-law!'

She caught up with Shiva on the darkened footpath that led to the edge of the mountain. He was going back to Kailash as he could not tolerate being out of isolation for so long.

'Yes, Lakshmi? What is it?' He was fond of her, just as Narayana was fond of Sati.

Lakshmi suddenly became shy. Her hands wrung together, and her toes curled in nervousness, setting her pretty bracelets and anklets tinkling. Truly, her beauty was infinite. 'I know you do not care for appearances. But this will be the most important day in Sati's life. For her sake—and her mother's—it would be nice, well...' Lakshmi's voice trailed off uncertainly.

'Well, what is it?'

Lakshmi straightened her spine and met his gaze squarely. 'Of course, you are Mahadeva, and the ash you smear across your body, the snake you drape around your neck, the tangled mass of locks you call your hair—all that is very well and good for a deva of your stature. But if you are truly beyond the duality of good and bad, life and death, beauty and horror, then it also would not detract from your glory if for one day you were to appear as an elegant, conventionally handsome bridegroom. Sati would never ask it of you, but I think you would do it to make her happy, just for one day.'

Shiva laughed uproariously, rustling the leaves surrounding them in the inky darkness with the vibrations of his chuckles. He winked at Lakshmi. 'Do not worry, Devi. I will look so beautiful that I will put your husband to shame.'

♋

Sati stood at the doorway, watching without being able to hear the banter between Shiva and Lakshmi. She smiled and looked back over her shoulder at Saraswati, remarking happily, 'I'm glad they are getting along.'

Saraswati's face was blank. 'Hmm,' was all she said.

'What is it, Saraswati? You do not approve of my marriage to Shiva?'

'It is not for me to approve or disapprove. I am devoted to knowledge and knowledge alone. The clear light of wisdom has no preferences or wishes. All I wish for, sister, is that you do whatever you do with your eyes open, in full and clear understanding of the consequences and meaning of each action, each decision you make.'

'I know who Shiva is, and I love him.' Sati's voice was firm.

Saraswati held up two graceful arms, wrapped in the pale-yellow silk of her sari. 'And do you not also love your father? And this *loka*, where all of us live together, your family?'

'Of course, I do! How dare you even suggest otherwise?'

'The two cannot coexist.'

'Of course, they can. They have for millions of years.'

'Yes, Shiva has his place, and this is another. Rarely do the two meet or mingle. But now you have brought both into collision with each other. And one day you may have to choose between them.'

Sati turned away from her sister. 'Nonsense. You always look at things negatively.' Yet she could not dismiss the niggling sense of foreboding that chilled her spine.

Saraswati walked up to Sati and hugged her. 'Do not be upset, sister. I want everything to work out well for you. Just be careful. And be thoughtful. The worst decisions are the decisions we never intended to make.'

♋

After their wedding on Mount Meru, Shiva quickly shooed away the guests. Only Nandi and Dawon remained behind. Shiva bent to whisper into Nandi's ear. Nandi gave Dawon a meaningful look, and then they both trotted away.

Sati looked at Shiva in surprise.

He took her by the elbow and said, 'Today, I will take you myself.'

And there was no travel, no lag in time, nothing, as Shiva instantly transported them to the lofty peaks of Kailash. They were high above the ground where the *ganas* lived, high above the plateau where Shiva received the occasional guests, on the snowy, icy summit where no one but Shiva had lived until now. Gusts of wind showered them with droplets of snow and ice, and from either side of the precipice, one could see entire galaxies revolving, the push and pull of life and death playing out like a mesmerising dance.

There was a cave, a dark, warm, cosy cave that Shiva called home, and it was no less magnificent than Narayana's opulent palace in Vaikuntha. It was just different, and Sati felt there had never been another place where she so belonged and felt at home, where she felt safe, protected and loved. But she would think of all that later. For now, there was nothing for Shiva and Sati but each other— seeing, touching, feeling each other, lost in each other's existence. They tumbled into an embrace, a kiss, a joining, intent on never letting go.

CHAPTER 10

A few million years passed before Shiva reluctantly pulled himself away from Sati's embrace. As with anything he did, his intensity and passion were unparalleled and unmatchable. Shiva sat up and immediately fell into a deep meditation.

Sati began foraging for food to cook a meal. She suddenly felt ravenous. Hunger was not something that afflicted her or the other devas and devis often, but once in a while, the craving for food appeared. And it had been a long, long time since she had spent with Shiva in passionate embrace. She tied her long hair into a loose topknot and draped herself in a rough-spun green dress she rapidly wove together. Her wedding sari had long since disintegrated into a tangle of threadbare silk. In Mount Meru, she would have had hundreds of maids to dress and decorate her. But Kailash was too bleak and desolate for any of them to have followed.

Sati did not mind as she stepped outside the cave and looked at her reflection in a patch of ice. She could no longer see in herself the pampered daughter of Daksha Prajapati. Now she appeared more as a yogini in penance. She stretched out her arms, bereft of any jewelled bracelets or rings, her cheeks untouched by any cosmetic powders or pastes, and felt deliciously free.

Nandi thundered up the mountainside, screeching to a halt at her feet. He looked at her with wide, eager eyes. She patted his head affectionately. 'Where is Dawon?' He bent his ear down to the ground to indicate that her lion was waiting for her there. Sati understood that only Nandi and she were allowed up to the top of Kailash in addition to Shiva.

Nandi gazed wistfully at the cave's entrance. How much he must have been missing Shiva, but Shiva was lost to meditation once again. Sati sympathised with him. Since before they had married, Sati sometimes feared that she would lose Shiva to meditation one day and he would not return to her.

Sati tried to distract him. 'Nandi, I wanted to cook something. Can we find any vegetables here?'

Nandi cocked his head at her sceptically, raising a hoof to indicate the vast expanse of snow and ice surrounding them.

'Well, there must be herbs or leaves or something. I, for one, am starving. What do all of you eat?'

Nandi said somberly, 'We feel no hunger when we are in the presence of our master. We are in his ambit, so if he does not eat, we don't feel the need to as well. The blessings of his meditation are all the nourishment we need. Even in meditation, he is always protecting and watching over us.'

Sati pressed her hand on her flat stomach and said wryly, 'I am in his ambit, too, but I suppose I am not yet fully under his protection since I am definitely suffering from hunger right now.'

Nandi said stiffly, 'He has been protecting you for a long time, without your even knowing it. He has been waiting for you since before you were born.'

Sati was startled by that revelation and wanted to ask more, but at that moment, Shiva emerged from the cave.

'Sati, is something wrong?' His voice was sleepy.

Sati turned around to face him. Though she had not left his arms for millions of years, her eyes were still greedy for the sight of him. 'I thought you were meditating? Did I disturb you?'

He came to her side and rustled her hair lovingly while giving Nandi his hand to sniff.

'How can I meditate if my wife is feeling hungry?' His eyes shone with bright amusement.

She asked, 'Is there really no food anywhere in Kailash?'

'Of course, there is. It's just a little far away.'

Sati turned towards Nandi, who looked back at her innocently. 'Nandi, you said that there was no food anywhere here.'

Shiva's booming laugh rang out. 'He was teasing you. This is what my *ganas* do all the time. Do not take it to heart.'

Sati's heart sank, daunted at the thought of how to win over the affection of the *ganas*. It had been hard enough to win the heart of Shiva.

Shiva took Sati by the arm and walked back into the cave, tossing a command back at Nandi to prepare their meal. As they waited, they watched the sun set from the opening of the cave. It was a lovely scene, with the pink rays of the sun sparkling on the snow-covered peaks that ranged out as far as the eye could see.

Shiva pulled Sati back into his chest, playing with her hair. She was unnerved that there were no signs of life here, no birds flying in the sky, no insects chirping on the ground, no vegetation straggling through the snow towards the sun. Shiva read her mind and dropped his chin onto her shoulder.

He cleared his throat. 'I have never spoken of such things to anyone before, but now that we are married, I must share my innermost thoughts and feelings with you, my dear. I hope you do not mind listening to my ramblings.'

Sati smiled and nestled deeper into his chest. Those 'ramblings' from this husband to his wife were the source of the most sacred and profound mystical tracts ever recorded. Those conversations carried forth the teachings of Shiva, the Adi Yogi, to the world.

At Sati's nod, Shiva started speaking thoughtfully. 'Ultimately, there is only Purusha and Prakriti. Purusha is the male principle, uncreated, absolute, unmanifest, passive consciousness, totally inert. On the other, Prakriti is represented by you, Sati, the force of creation, dynamic, kinetic and the giver of all life. The material world is your play as the unfurling of Prakriti, whereas here in my abode—now our abode—Kailash represents Purusha and Purusha alone.

'Because I am untouched by Prakriti, because I am unconcerned with any part of the material world, Prakriti does not contaminate Kailash.'

'Contaminate?' Sati's eyebrows shot up, which Shiva missed, wrapped up as he was in his discourse.

'Emotions, clothes, home and shelter, food—all these come under maya and have no reality and no importance.

That is why you do not see birds flying here or hear the chirping of insects. Here it is pure, untainted consciousness and consciousness alone that prevails. Purusha and Purusha alone.'

Sati said softly, 'But I am not Purusha.' She remembered what Brhaspati had once taught her about balance the first day she had seen Shiva. Perhaps it was time for him to realise the same, too. A mischievous smile curled her lips.

At that moment, Nandi appeared, with a large, steaming copper vessel brimming full of a savoury *khichdi* strapped across his back.

Shiva sniffed the air appreciatively. 'That smells good!'

Sati cast a sidelong glance at her husband. 'But it is Prakriti!'

He raised a brow. 'Prakriti is okay to enjoy when it is here. I certainly appreciate it.' He shrugged. 'I am just unaffected by it and not dependent on it.'

As Shiva reached to unstrap the food from Nandi's back, Sati snatched the vessel from his hands and instantaneously disappeared.

Nandi's jaw dropped as he looked at Shiva in alarm. 'What happened to Devi? Is she okay? Why did she disappear?'

Shiva frowned. 'I think I have upset my wife, Nandi.'

Nandi moved his head this way and that, looking for Sati. 'Shouldn't we try to find her?'

Shiva smiled cryptically. 'If my wife does not wish to be found, I will not be able to find her. It is beyond my power.'

Nandi sighed heavily.

'Do not worry. I am sure she will come back as soon as she is a little calmer.'

Nandi pawed the ground. *I am a celibate bull, but it looks like even I know more about marriage than you.*

Shiva settled himself into meditation once again. Within the space of a few hours, a loud chorus of wailing from the *ganas* below roused him. It was nearing midnight. Shiva came out of the cave and descended to the bottom of the mountain, where the *ganas* were gnashing their teeth and stomping the ground petulantly. He bit back a smile. The *ganas*, as frightening as they were in appearance, often behaved like overgrown children.

When he asked them what the matter was, Nandi reported that they were hungry but there was no food to be found in all of Kailash. Shiva closed his eyes to investigate, surveying the topography of the snowy planet in his mind's eye. He realised that when Sati had left, she had taken all of Prakriti with her, rendering the planet barren.

Shiva sighed. He had no practice in dealing with women and pacifying their feelings. He had hoped she would come back on her own when she felt like it, and until then he could rest in his meditation. But to his surprise, he discovered that he missed her.

He turned to the *ganas*. 'It has only been a few hours. If you would only concentrate on the knowledge that you are not this body, you will not feel hunger. I have not eaten in so many millions of years, but I feel no thirst or hunger.' *The only thing I miss is my wife*, he thought.

The *ganas* looked at him doubtfully. Still, they were obedient to him and dutifully tried to identify themselves as separate and distinct from their bodies. It was endearing to see this motley assortment of giants and malformed beings sitting as quietly as they could, some belching, others scratching their bare bellies, some yawning with more holes in their gums than teeth. Despite their sincere efforts, their stomachs grumbled in protest.

Shiva told them to wait while he tried to rustle up some food for them. He wandered from planet to planet in search of food. He started with Earth since mortals there tended to be kind and sharing. But the households there were bereft of food, too. He went to visit his friend Kubera in the neighbouring Alakapuri. Kubera was the deva of wealth. But even he was despondent and hungry, unable to exchange his hoard of treasures for even a gram of food, as all vegetation, all sources of nourishment, had vanished with Sati.

Finally, Shiva went to Vaikuntha. Because of his special status, he did not have to go through the doors guarded by Jaya and Vijaya, the two gatekeepers to Narayana's abode. He promptly appeared in the visiting chambers of Lakshmi and Narayana, where they were enjoying the singing of a troupe of *gandharvas*.

Narayana grinned at his appearance. With a wave of his hands, Narayana dismissed the *gandharvas*, emptying the chamber so that only the three of them remained.

'Shiva! I had begun to think you were never coming back. You have been gone for so long.' He turned to his wife. 'Isn't marriage suiting him well, Devi? He seems to be glowing.'

Lakshmi scowled. 'It's suiting him fine, but why is my sister so upset?'

Shiva's ears perked up. 'Is Sati here?' His eyes scanned the palace.

'No! But I cannot feel her presence, and I am always able to feel her vibrations. She must be really unhappy. That's why you have come, isn't it?' Her eyes narrowed.

'Actually, I have come to get food for my *ganas*, who are hungry. I thought there must be food in Vaikuntha, if nowhere else. I'm sure Sati will feel better soon and come back. Don't worry. She has been quite happy with me.'

Lakshmi closed her eyes, and when she opened them again a few moments later, they were wide and troubled. 'I am the source of all plenitude, but it is Sati who is the cause of all material existence. Without her, there is no food nor any seeds or sources of food. She has withdrawn not only herself but also all her powers.'

'Sati is being too dramatic, really. We were just having a simple discussion.'

'About what?'

'About how I am Purusha and untainted by the need of anything material, untouched by concern over food, water, heat or cold, dry or wet. She need not have taken it personally. My love for her has nothing to do with her material powers. I love her for her.'

Lakshmi's voice turned acerbic. 'Who says she is taking it personally? You were trying to teach her a lesson. Maybe she is teaching you one now.'

Shiva grinned with delight. He had not anticipated that even quarrelling with his wife could be so intriguing. There were indeed benefits to marriage he had not considered before.

At that moment, the great sage Narada was ushered in by Jaya and Vijaya. 'Narayana, Narayana!' Narada chanted as he swept past Shiva and fell in prostration to Narayana.

He offered his bows to Lakshmi and Shiva. 'It is good you are here, Mahadeva!' Narada exclaimed in relief. 'I think we will need your help with this one, too. All the worlds are in great distress, O devas! Everyone is suffering from hunger and the harsh climates of worlds, suddenly transformed into arid deserts or barren wastelands. There is such great misery in the world. The humans and other mortals still live, but all sources of their nourishment have disappeared.'

'It is because my wife has disappeared,' said Shiva. 'Have you heard or seen her anywhere in your travels here?' Narada was a great rishi, who, due to a curse, was not able to stay in any place for longer than a few minutes. He travelled the worlds incessantly, eternally chanting the name of Narayana. His constant travels made him a great source of information, and fortunately, Narada was a great fan of gossip. He was also a troublemaker who liked to meddle in people's affairs and instigate intriguing contests and dilemmas that ended up being solved by Narayana.

'Hmm... No. But they say there is a devi in a remote corner of a forest somewhere on Earth, near the banks of the Ganga. She is giving out food to those who come to visit her.'

It could be no one else but Sati. Shiva immediately vanished to find her.

Narada was surprised. Usually, Shiva was indifferent to the affairs of the mortals. He said to Narayana, 'Shiva? Why did he go? Aren't you going to fix this problem?'

Narayana laughed. 'He got us all into this pickle. He can solve it himself.'

Lakshmi nodded emphatically.

♋

Shiva transformed himself into a beggar and wandered across Earth. Bowl in hand, he went from house to house, searching for Sati. There was a great darkness on the land. People had stopped farming. Without the sacrificial offerings, the yajnas had come to a halt. There were no rains. Only the passing of the sun across the skies. There were no flowers, no leaves on trees to provide shade from the sweltering heat. The birds, the bees, the insects, the mortals, all were struggling. It had hardly been a day since Sati had disappeared, but already so much havoc had been wrought.

As he wandered along the banks of the Ganga, he heard about the benevolent devi who was feeding everyone who came to her abode. As he approached that place, he could see streams of people fanning out from the simply built wooden hall where she was sitting. Crowds thronged, bowls in hand, for her alms.

Shiva joined them, waiting patiently in line. Finally, when he entered the wooden enclosure, even as he expected to see his wife, he was amazed at the sight of her. She sat resplendent upon a golden throne, garbed in scarlet silk, in one hand a golden spoon with which she filled the bowls of those who came before her, in the other a golden vessel full of an ambrosial rice-and-milk preparation that was never depleted. Shiva noticed that as people emerged from the chamber, gobbling their way quickly to the bottom of their bowls, the food magically replenished until they ate their fill.

Shiva knew as soon as he saw her that this devi was indeed his Sati. Whatever form she took, he would always recognise her. When it was his turn, he stood before her not as her husband or Mahadeva, but as a simple beggar holding out a roughly hewn wooden bowl. Her eyes were full of love and kindness, overflowing with compassion and warmth, as if they had never quarrelled. And he understood then that she could not bear for anyone to suffer from hunger, even for a few hours, that as quickly as she had taken herself away, she had come back to feed one and all alike. At this rate, the whole world would be at her feet in no time, waiting to be fed by her hands.

As he bowed to her, she filled his bowl generously, lovingly. The moment their eyes met and Shiva's bowl was filled, all vegetation and life returned to all the worlds, all the pantries overflowed, all begging bowls brimmed with food, all gardens and farms became fertile and ready for harvest. All hunger disappeared from the world for a time. Shiva's disguise as a beggar fell away. The people around them fell in prostration to him and Sati as they realised who they were. Shiva lifted a finger and transformed the simple wooden hall into an opulent temple with a marble floor and ornate golden decorations. Shiva himself worshipped Sati in this unique form, a form that had never been seen before. He called her Annapurna, the bestower of food and nourishment. The temple would remain through the ravages of time to honour her as Annapurna Devi.

After everyone else disappeared, they spent some time wandering through the beautiful forest along the banks of the river. Sati filled her arms with wildflowers, which Shiva braided into her hair. Some he tucked behind his own ears. Shiva noticed how entranced Sati was by this place.

'This could be our second home, you know,' he offered.

This took Sati by surprise. 'Here? In a mortal world?' she asked.

Shiva shrugged. 'Why not? What inch of this universe is not sacred, after all? There is a kind of peacefulness and stillness here, even though it is not in the mountains. And the Ganga is here, which makes it special.' He fingered his hair, affectionately remembering the sacred river that flowed through his tresses. 'And now this has a special memory for us. I understand Kailash may not always be... what you are in the mood for. And I am equally happy here. So, let this be our home, too.'

In time, that wild forest would transform into the city of Varanasi, or Kashi, the sacred city of Shiva, the holiest city in all the worlds.

Later, Shiva and Sati returned to Kailash. All the *ganas* shouted in joy, relieved that Sati had returned. They bowed to her deeply and most respectfully, grateful that she had made Kailash so fertile that their bellies would be ever full and content.

'They appear to venerate you more than they do me,' Shiva remarked.

Sati's heart squeezed as she looked at the *ganas*. Once they had seemed so repugnant and fearsome to her, but now they were her very own family, and this her own home.

The Earth they had left behind had also changed. People learned to treasure each grain of rice as a gem. The preparation and offering of food, the very process of feeding, became a sacred act. So long as that memory remained—of having been fed by a devi herself, of her compassion and generosity—eating and cooking would not be taken for granted.

As Shiva led Sati back to their cave, he asked her softly, 'Are you still upset with me?'

'I was never upset, to begin with. I was teaching you a lesson, just as you were trying to teach me. You use abstract words and metaphors, dense and arcane tracts of philosophy. I use simple examples and actions to prove my point.'

Shiva grinned. 'That's exactly what Lakshmi said.' He then described his exchanges with Narayana and Lakshmi.

Sati smiled sleepily as he held her to his chest. 'So, they teased you about being a newly-wed husband, hmm? I suppose we are not so different from mortals after all.'

Shiva snuggled her more tightly as he closed his eyes. 'The difference is when mortal couples argue, they produce anger and other negative feelings. But we created a new devi.'

And almost starved the world, thought Sati, but she did not say it aloud. She liked her husband's interpretation better.

CHAPTER 11

A nd just like that, many more years passed in bliss and love. They spent their time in Kailash, in Kashi and in wandering the Himalayas, a place they found particularly beautiful and conducive for meditation or to simply while away some time. They frequented their favourite spots in other worlds, too.

Sati could never forget Saraswati's words of warning, though, or Bhrigu's omen of foreboding about seeing death in her marriage. As happy as she was, she could not shake the feeling that it would not last, that something terrible was about to happen. And then, one day, it did.

One afternoon, Sati was sitting on the mountainside of Kailash, weaving flowers into wreaths to decorate their cave. She saw a *vimana*, an aerial chariot, soaring through the skies. She squinted up and saw Rohini, one of her many sisters, waving at her. Sati waved and beckoned her to come down.

The *vimana* zoomed down, and Rohini descended with her husband, Chandra, the moon deva. Sati hugged Rohini tightly. She had not seen anyone from her family for aeons. Her ethereal beauty of a sister was as light as a leaf in her arms. The meeting left her awash in homesickness and longing for her family.

She then exchanged pleasantries with her brother-in-law. Chandra was sheepish, as he was any time he encountered anybody in the company of his wife. It was well-known throughout Devaloka that, of his twenty-seven wives—all of whom were Sati's sisters—Rohini was his favourite. It had been a festering scandal among the devas, as were Chandra's insatiable appetites. The devas had gone to war with him to bring Tara back from his clutches to her husband, Brhaspati. It was then that he had married Sati's twenty-seven sisters to forget Tara. But now Tara appeared to have been replaced by Rohini, spawning tension and jealousy between Rohini and her sisters.

Chandra stammered, 'Err, well, we were on our way to a yajna and thought we would take this shortcut as we are running late. Shiva had granted me permission to travel through the skies here if needed.'

Sati knew Shiva had a soft spot for Chandra. He was one of the few among Sati's relatives whom Shiva liked. When Rohini's sisters had gone complaining to their father, Daksha had cursed Chandra to wane and shrink to nothing in fourteen days. Chandra had begun to shrink day by day. On the fourteenth day, when he had been diminished to a sliver of a crescent, he had begged Shiva for help.

Shiva calmly picked him up and placed Chandra in his hair. So, adorning Shiva, Chandra's beauty in this form would be preserved forever and could not be reached by Daksha's curse. Moreover, Shiva blessed Chandra that he would wax for fourteen days and attain his full glory on the fifteenth day. But, since Daksha's curse had to be given its due, Chandra would then wane again into nothing and then rise and fall again and again, without end. From then onward, Shiva had borne the crescent moon in his hair until he had bestowed it upon Sati.

Truly, reflected Sati, *there was no one more generous in giving blessings and rescuing beings from assorted troubles than Shiva.* He was even called Bholenath because of his unrestrained kindness. His heart was easily won despite his ferocious appearance. Sati knew there was another side to him, the dangerous, destructive dance of anger and annihilation. She had not witnessed it yet and hoped she never would.

'Which yajna are you attending?' Sati asked absent-mindedly, lost in thoughts of her husband.

When both Chandra and Rohini hesitated, glancing at each other uneasily, Sati's attention focused on them. 'Which yajna are you attending?' she repeated slowly, firmly, in a voice that brooked no argument. This was the voice of Durga, and none dared resist.

'Our father is having a yajna in Kankhal,' Rohini whispered.

Sati's brow wrinkled. 'I did not see any invitation.' She asked Nandi if he had seen any such invitation. He shook his head gravely, a troubled expression clouding his face, as if he could see what was going to happen but could not stop it.

'Sati...he did not send you an invitation,' whispered Rohini softly. Her black eyes were luminous and huge in her narrow, oval face, as fair and golden as her husband's countenance. 'Perhaps he thought you were busy. After all, you have not been back to Mount Meru since your wedding, other than on the nights of Shivaratri. And everyone is so lost in meditation then, we do not even see each other.'

Sati stood up, bristling. 'Nonsense! I am his daughter. I am Dakshayani. Of course, I must have been invited. There must have been some mistake, that's all.'

Chandra's face tightened as if he could see there was an impending storm and he wanted to get away as quickly as possible. 'Come, Rohini, we will be late.'

Rohini hugged Sati one last time. 'Don't worry, Sati. Even if you do not come to the yajna, we can all still meet. Come home, dear. We all miss you. At least come for a visit.'

They left, and Sati felt cold and bereft, tears pricking her eyes. She was flooded with memories of her girlhood home, her family, Lakshmi, Saraswati, the comforting assemblies of the devas, rishis and others for the various yajnas and ceremonies.

'Kankhal,' Sati said to herself. To add salt to the wound, it was a place that Shiva and she frequented near the foothills of the Himalayas, near the banks of the Ganga.

Sati entered the cave where Shiva was meditating. His eyes opened immediately as he could sense her distress.

Sati told him, 'My father is hosting a yajna in Kankhal.'

Shiva nodded. 'Yes, so?'

Sati's mouth fell open. 'You knew about this? And you did not tell me?'

Shiva rubbed the backs of his eyes, a little impatiently. 'What is the sense of talking about it? He hosts yajnas all the time.'

'But this is a special one. All the devas have been invited.'

'Except for me.'

An uncomfortable silence hung between them for the first time since their marriage. 'I am his daughter. He should not have to invite us. He would never turn me away. How can it be that Chandra, the son-in-law he has cursed, is attending but you are not?'

Shiva sighed. 'Sati, there is much I do not tell you. You know my very presence rankles your father. He has never been in favour of our marriage. Even before we married, your father and I disagreed on many different issues. It is good enough that for your sake we are not in an open war. He has made it a point not to invite me this time. It is known to all. I did not want to hurt you. I know he is your family. You are free to visit with them and spend time on Mount Meru whenever you want. But do not ask me to go to a yajna where I am not invited.'

Sati shook her head. 'He can be stubborn sometimes. But he will listen to me. He always listens to me. I am his favourite daughter. Let me go and fix the situation, even if you will not come with me.'

'Sati, do not go.' His voice was placid yet implacable. It was the closest he had come to issuing her a command in all their time together.

She shook her head. 'This is not acceptable. You are Mahadeva. You are my husband. I am his daughter. Why should we be estranged? For so long, there has been only silence between us. I will not let it be like this.' She pleaded with her husband. 'I know what you think of him. But you do not know how much he loves me. He will not hurt me.'

Shiva closed his eyes for a moment and when he opened them, there was a hardness Sati had not seen before. What he saw in his mystical vision he did not share in that moment with his wife. He simply said, 'If you go, it will force things into a crisis. There will be no coming back.'

There was an intensity in his gaze that held Sati even as she tried to look away. Her heart skipped a beat. Perhaps it was the nostalgia triggered by seeing her sister, the years of longing for and missing her family and friends back home or the indignation of having been rejected by her father. Whatever it was, she was not able to back down.

'My father and my husband cannot be enemies. Saraswati warned me at the time of our wedding that the situation was untenable unless I faced the truth and took responsibility for it. She was right. I must go and make things right.'

Shiva was silent for a time. It was not in his nature to argue or impose his will on anybody, including his wife. It was not in his nature to repeat himself. He believed in the paramount place of free will. He was not the one to stop anybody from following their heart. He saw the homesickness and heartache in his wife's face and knew her decision had been made.

His voice was neutral as he said, 'Take Nandi with you and all the *ganas*.'

'All of them?' she asked in surprise.

'Yes, every single one. They will protect you.'

She laughed uneasily. 'Protect me? From my father?'

Shiva did not reply. *Not from your father. Who in this cosmos could pose a threat to you, after all? From your own heartbreak.*

Sati walked away. At the entrance of the cave, she stood for a few moments. Then, she turned towards him with a wistful smile, bathed in the golden and crimson hues of the setting sun.

'I will come back soon. If I come with his invitation, you will go with me to the yajna, won't you?'

He did not respond. Saying yes would have been meaningless, a falsity, responding to something that could never come true, an impossibility, like a rabbit with horns or the son of a barren woman. Above all, he was Shivam Satyam Sundaram, auspicious, truthful and beautiful, and he could not betray that, not even for Sati.

Sati turned away. 'I will come back soon,' she repeated.

Shiva watched wordlessly as she left him, knowing he would never see her again.

♋

For hours, Shiva sat immobile, looking at the empty spot where Sati had stood. Then, a fluttering of Garuda's wings heralded the arrival of Narayana. Shiva went to greet him. 'What are you doing here?'

Narayana rarely came to visit Kailash. Hardly anyone did.

'I am on my way to Daksha's yajna. I heard that Sati is going, too.'

'Ah, so you are also going.'

'Well, Daksha has always been devoted to me so I cannot refuse him. Isn't this the trap we always fall into, Shiva? Everyone thinks we are the most powerful devas in the universe, and of course, we are. They think we can do whatever we want. But *bhavagrahi janardana*—we are beholden to our devotees. And this is how we get stuck in situations we would like to avoid.'

Shiva nodded. 'Yes, I understand. In any event, I am glad you will be there. I want you to look out for Sati.'

Narayana snorted. 'As if that is something to be asked. Do you think my wife would forgive me if anything were to happen to her beloved sister? Do you think I would forgive myself?'

Shiva settled on his deerskin mat and closed his eyes. 'True. I forget she is beloved to all of us.'

Narayana sat before him, pensive, waiting until Shiva opened his eyes. Narayana's face was uncharacteristically grave as he said softly, 'All the same, Shiva, I think you should come. I am worried. And I rarely worry.'

Shiva turned his head. 'Nandi is with her. All my *ganas* are with her. Who can touch her? If she needs me, she need only think of me and immediately I will be by her side.'

Narayana's voice became urgent. 'You know as I do just how dangerous this can become. Who Daksha is. Who she is. Come with me. Everyone knows he was wrong not to invite you. We will kill him on the spot for the insult and end this once and for all.'

'We cannot kill Sati's father unprovoked. Go, Narayana. You know as well as I do there is nothing to be done. My place is here, in Kailash, alone.'

There was something terrible and resolute in his voice.

Narayana reluctantly got up and walked away.

'Do not worry about Sati,' said Shiva. 'She is under my protection. Always.'

Narayana mounted Garuda and his words became almost indistinct amidst the fluttering of the great eagle's winged ascent into the skies.

'It is not Sati I am worried about. It is you.'

Dusk had just set in when Sati landed in Kankhal. She instructed the *ganas* to stay at the borders of the *yajnashala*, the constructed enclosure for the yajna. She knew others would be wary of them. She had thought she would spend time with her mother and sisters first, that she would bathe in the river with Lakshmi and Saraswati, that she would visit her favourite rishis and make her prostrations to them.

But now that she was here, all she could think of was her father and righting the wrong he was committing. All she could think of was Shiva. She missed him already. If Shiva had been here, he would have guided her through the crowds, whispered amusing things into her ear, kept her hand warmly in his. He would have brought her delight in every moment, as he always had. He indulged her whims and desires, let her be as she wanted to be. He had never asked anything of her.

Sati, do not go.

She winced at the memory of those words. With every step forward, she wanted to run back to their home, where none dared to disturb them. Where she belonged.

Perhaps she would have turned back were it not for what she saw at that moment. She broke through the crowds to reach the fire altar, where the yajna had already commenced. All the devas were there, every single one. Narayana, Indra, Chandra, Mitra, Pushan, Agni, Vayu, Varuna...only Shiva was missing. It looked so wrong, was so wrong, that Sati could not bear it. The devas without Shiva were incomplete.

Her teeth gnashed together. Her hair loosened from their ties and fell across her trembling shoulders in long, dark tresses.

As she saw her father and all the devas seated there, all carrying on without Shiva in his rightful place, her voice thundered, 'How dare you conduct this sacrifice without giving my husband his share? No blessings can come without his presence, without him receiving his due.'

Daksha lifted his face slowly to confront his daughter. Sati nearly gasped at the sight of him. In their years apart, he had grown haggard, stouter, his cheekbones sunken, dark spots covering his bearded face.

His voice sputtered with rage. 'That Shiva is nothing but a barbarian. I regret the day I let you marry him. It is enough if Narayana is here. Shiva is not needed. I refuse to give him a single grain of rice as an offering! What a disgusting, uncouth creature, unfit to be among this hallowed pantheon of devas!'

Sati gritted her teeth. Outside, the *ganas* grew restless and troubled as they could feel her anguish. Her voice turned cold. 'Yes, it is true, my husband sits on the cremation ground with dishevelled hair. It is true he wears a garland of skulls. It is true that he smears the ashes of the dead on his body. But it is also true that all the devas, all the rishis, all the wise ones of the worlds take the dust of his feet humbly on their heads.'

She could not bear to look at her father or any of the other devas there, not even Narayana, not even her beloved guru, Brhaspati. None dared to approach her. Her anger was so incandescent that they sat immobile, terrified of her. Her eyes fell in an unfocused gaze onto the sacrificial fire, the only pure thing in that entire enclosure. She blinked back tears as she remembered Shiva, her husband and their life together.

'Give him his share of the sacrifice.' She spoke as a devi.

Daksha sneered at her and returned his attention to the yajna, muttering chants and offering oblations into the fire. He acted as if she did not exist. The devas, her mother, her sisters, the rishis...no one said a word.

Sati stood there in silence, realising she had failed. And in failing, she had allowed her husband to be insulted in her presence. She could not go back. She could never go back. She could not live having disgraced him.

Sati's voice gained force and volume, ricocheting across the pillars of the *yajnashala*. 'My husband fondly calls me Dakshayani, the daughter of Daksha, as a mark of respect for you. But I renounce you and all those who have gathered here today. I am no longer your daughter. I am no longer fit to be called by any name at all.'

It was said that fire was the great purifier. Sati gathered herself into her body, retreating from the world. Once, many years ago, she had withdrawn herself and all her powers, and Shiva had come to her with a begging bowl to bring her back. This time, she was going where none could bring her back.

She thought only of Shiva as she slowed her breathing. She sought to control her mind, to go into a state of meditation as Shiva did. She had to do this the right way, not in a pique of anger or grief. She closed her eyes. She could feel the flames of the sacrificial fire fattening with the offerings of ghee made by the officiating brahmanas.

'It is not a pure enough offering, the hollow oblations made out of greed, arrogance and pride, made without remembrance of Shiva. If still my father wants this yajna to be completed, let there be one worthy offering at least.'

Sati sank to a seated position, facing the northern direction. In the faint fringes of her consciousness, she could hear Saraswati and Lakshmi cry out and run towards her, but she repelled them. At the moment of her choosing, she became lifeless. Some said her body fell into the sacrificial fire. Others said she jumped into the flames. Nobody was able to remember it properly.

As the devas yelled out in shock and horror, the *ganas* howled in distress and fury. They ran through the *yajnashala*, shrieking in ghoulish, shrill tones. They hacked to pieces all creatures who lay in their path; some even cut off their own limbs in their insensible grief.

Bhrigu and the other rishis grew alarmed. With the power of the mantras they muttered, hundreds of thousands of warriors emerged from the still-smouldering sacrificial fire and began fighting with the *ganas*. The fire burned bright and hot, illuminating in macabre, jagged rays of light the masses of *ganas* fighting with the armies of the rishi-born soldiers. Twenty thousand *ganas* died in the first moments of the battle. Soon enough, they were routed, but the violent warring continued as devas and rishis writhed in pain on the ground, their limbs, noses, ears having been lopped off by the *ganas*. The devas began despairing.

Narayana was ashen-faced. He tried to hold back the *ganas* without killing them. It was a half-hearted fight on his part; he knew they fought only out of grief and love for Shiva and Sati. The entire fight was senseless, caused by Daksha's blind hate. He diverted the flames of the sacrificial fire away from Sati's body so it did not get charred into ash. He did not dare touch her himself.

CHAPTER 12

Shiva sat in meditation in Kailash. The moment Sati left her body, his eyes opened. He was motionless until the *ganas* came to him, pleading for his help to save them from defeat at the hands of the devas and rishis. He plucked a hair from his head. That piece of hair was transformed into Virabhadra, the fiercest *gana* ever, a manifestation of Rudra himself. From the angry breath of Shiva came different forms of fevers and plagues. He manifested thousands of *ganas*. He sent the yoginis, the fiercest of devis, like Bhadrakali and others, to destroy the yajna of Daksha once and for all.

Virabhadra began the march back to Kankhal. His footsteps ushered grievous omens for the devas. Constellations began swirling in never-before-seen formations. Stars fell from their firmaments in blazing trails of fire. The devas began vomiting pieces of their own flesh and bones. Blood started raining from the sky. Earthquakes raged and whirlwinds of dust were raised by the fall of Virabhadra's feet.

When Virabhadra reached the *yajnashala*, he decapitated Daksha and burnt his head into a crisp in the sacrificial fire. He then began slaying the celestials without mercy.

All of Kankhal was overrun by the *ganas* and yoginis summoned by Shiva. The air rang with screams of anguish from the ravaged devas and rishis. As fast and as furiously as Virabhadra cut down the rishis' armies, the rishis created more. And as the soldiers decimated the *ganas*, more emerged. It was a stalemate.

The destruction was so great that eventually, Narayana had to step in.

The duel between Narayana and Virabhadra dragged on for a long time, wreaking damage on both sides, with no clear outcome in sight.

Shiva did not want to leave Kailash. If he allowed himself to act on even a quiver of the rage that burned within, all the worlds would wink out of existence. Yet he could not stay unmoved when there were cries for help bellowing out from the worlds that felt the unrest that Sati's death had wrought.

Just as Narayana reached for the Sudarshana Chakra, Shiva appeared in the middle of the *yajnashala*. He motioned for both Narayana and Virabhadra to stop.

'Let it be,' he said. 'There has been enough destruction and death.' Then he restored all the devas to their original forms. Only Daksha remained decapitated and Sati lifeless.

'Can you not bring her back?' Virabhadra asked.

'She is beyond my powers.' He stared at her body. Though she had cast herself into the sacrificial fire, her form was still intact and perfect, only the edges of her sari charred black.

Narayana said gently, 'The yajna cannot be left uncomplete. It must be finished. Shiva, please take your share and let the yajna resume.'

'Because you gave your word to your devotee, Daksha?'

Narayana shook his head. 'Not just that. Because the harmony and order of the universe depend on it. So much destruction has taken place in these few hours. We need to restore balance.'

'So be it,' said Shiva. He replaced Daksha's head with that of a goat. 'Let him finish the yajna this way.'

Shiva turned away from the devas. He carefully picked up Sati's corpse, cradling it against his chest, and walked out of the *yajnashala*. As he held her, he was flooded with memories of their life together. All the places they had roamed, all their teasing banter, their conversations about the mystical and supernatural, their warm embraces. He had sealed Kailash when he had left for Kankhal behind an impenetrable barrier to keep it safe from interlopers. But he would not be going back there.

As he emerged from the *yajnashala*, Nandi came up to him, sniffing Shiva's feet sadly. His fur was flecked with blood. He was so morose at the loss of Sati that he could not even meet Shiva's eyes. He brayed sadly, motioning for Shiva to climb on his back so that they could go home.

Shiva shook his head and walked away from Nandi. He wanted only Sati. He began walking in the skies, carrying Sati's corpse from one corner of the universe to the other. Overwhelmed with grief and longing for his wife, he roamed with her through their old haunts in the Himalayas, in the forests of Kashi. He carried her through the starry nights and blazing hot sun-filled desert skies. He walked with her through glaciers and the calm, soothing seas. Not for a moment did he stop. He wanted to show Sati all of the worlds in all their glory, things she had never seen, things they had not seen together.

♋

Thousands of years passed like this. One day, in Vaikuntha, Lakshmi said to Narayana, 'You have to stop him. He cannot go on this way. My poor sister's body—even now, she is not getting any peace. He has to let her go, so she can also find peace.'

Narayana sighed. 'I know. I do not want to disturb him. I thought he would let her go in time. But his grief is unending.'

All of Devaloka was still mired in sorrow at the loss of Sati. Vasant, the season of spring, had passed without the customary merriment. Indra and Shachi eschewed the feasts they normally hosted. The *gandharvas* sang only sad songs. The apsaras did not feel like dancing. Even Narayana had grown subdued. No one, other than Shiva, was more distressed than Lakshmi and the normally unflappable Saraswati.

Narayana reluctantly followed Shiva. For a long time, he said nothing, just trailed behind Shiva. The worlds beneath their feet were collapsing from the strength of Shiva's pain. The oceans were flooding the lands and volcanoes were sending streams of molten lava through villages and towns. The sun and moon were too afraid to rise and set. The universe was on the verge of *pralaya*, cyclical cosmic dissolution. But it was not yet time.

'I know you are there. How long will you follow me?' Shiva said in a raspy and broken voice.

They were on the fringes of the universe, many millions of light years away from any inhabited planets. Narayana faced Shiva. His heart dropped at the sight of Sati. She was golden and beautifully preserved in Shiva's arms, but it was jarring to see her as a listless body.

'You know you have to let her go.'

Shiva shrugged. 'After all, I am used to corpses. I will carry her through the rest of time.'

Narayana sighed. 'Time cannot withstand the force of your grief and sorrow. Time is collapsing. The entire srishti—all of creation—is coming to an end. The mortals are crying for relief. You must let her go.'

Shiva turned away. 'I am going far, far away where no one will feel me or be impacted by me.'

Narayana's voice sharpened. 'You are Mahadeva. Whatever you do, whatever you feel, all the mortals will be impacted.'

Shiva began moving faster, charging through the universe, evading Narayana's reach. But wherever he went, Narayana appeared in the next moment. Shiva growled and kept zooming away, but to no avail.

'Narayana, this is ridiculous. Go back.'

In response, he only heard the whirring of Narayana's Sudarshana Chakra.

Shiva stiffened. 'Do not do it.' He crushed Sati's body to his chest protectively. 'Sati was always frightened of your chakra for some reason. Do not do this to her.'

It had been an argument since time immemorial, whether Narayana was superior or Shiva. Idiotic questions have no answer. The reality was that there was a *rtam*, a balancing of the forces of the universe. And for that, Shiva's grief had to come to an end. The need of that hour was for Narayana to prevail.

Narayana was relentless. With a flick of his finger, he sent the chakra zinging into Sati's corpse, slicing through her body. Wherever Shiva went, Narayana was always in front of him. Parts of Sati's body fell here and there, consecrating those spots as sacred sites, where in time, temples would be established and dedicated to her. Soon, there was nothing left of Sati for Shiva to hold. All one hundred and eight pieces of her corpse had fallen to the ground. When the last remnant of her disappeared, the intense fire that had been consuming Shiva was put out, leaving him resigned and bereft.

He told Narayana, 'It is time I returned to my old ways.'

And then he disappeared and became lost in meditation in the icy caves of the Himalayas.

PART II

PARVATI

CHAPTER 13

How could life continue without its source? How could the universe go on without Sati? It could not. It was only a matter of time. But what an awful time that was. Without Sati, there was no turning of the seasons, no profusion of flowers in bloom or blowing of the winds. Rivers and oceans grew stagnant. The land was not barren but yielded only the bare minimum of crops, all of which tasted stale. People, animals, plants survived but did not flourish. Birds hopped mournfully from one branch to another but no longer sang. Trees bore leaves but no flowers. The world had forgotten the taste of fruit and vegetables.

The rishis were worried. Shiva had become so lost in meditation for these millions of years that he had started to miss Shivaratri at Mount Meru. It became a matter of debate in Devaloka. Should Shiva be permitted to remain like this or did he need to be roused? After all, some said, his natural state was isolation and meditation. He was just returning to his roots. Others fretted that he had become impervious even to the calls of the *ganas*. He had become lost to the world. And without him, they argued, the world would be lost, too.

And then it became political. Narada reported to Narayana and Lakshmi, as they rested in Vaikuntha, that there were some among the mortals and celestials who preferred having Shiva out of the way.

'What do you mean?' Lakshmi asked in surprise.

'Well... Shiva has always been a troublemaker. Rebellious, unpredictable, terrifying when angered. The devas all shudder before him. Whereas, you, Narayana... well, you are always so calm and peaceful. So stable. Some are wondering whether it is not better this way, after all. To preserve order and harmony. Leave Shiva undisturbed and, thus, let all others be undisturbed.'

Irritation flickered in Narayana's eyes. He said sharply, 'Sometimes the *srishti* could use a bit of disruption and rebellion. Sometimes chaos restores order. Sometimes the rules are meant to be broken to remind us of the transience and limitations of all rules, all restrictions, all definitions. It is when Shiva makes us the most uncomfortable that we most need him.'

Narada hummed sagely in agreement.

Lakshmi spoke, 'What can we do, though? You have already tried to visit him so many times. He does not respond to you, to Nandi or even to the *ganas*. How can he be woken?'

Narayana mentally ran through the usual tricks that worked on males, which mostly consisted of sending beautiful women and apsaras to tempt them and interrupt their meditation. Kamadeva, the deva of love, was particularly skilled at this. But he had irritated Shiva no end when his name was suggested earlier as a potential suitor for Sati, so Narayana was reluctant to call upon him. Yet.

He shrugged haplessly. 'It is beyond my powers right now.'

Lakshmi's face drooped in sadness. 'Only Sati could wake him. And she is gone.'

An inscrutable shadow darkened Narayana's blue face. Narada was about to ask him about it when Narayana sent him a signal to keep quiet. There was nothing that Narada loved more than secrets and stories, so he was practically hopping on his feet in anticipation the rest of the evening. Finally, when Lakshmi left to tend to the flowering gardens, Narada asked Narayana why he had looked so odd when Lakshmi had mentioned Sati.

Narayana's jaw tightened. 'I did not want to say anything in front of my wife because I am not yet certain, but I feel Sati may be back. It is rare that a devi or deva is born, and there is a great deal of formality around it. Usually, we would all know. This time, there was no news or announcement, but I feel a stirring in the air, the appearance of great power. What else could it be but Sati? I plan to investigate it but I want to keep it a secret for the time being.'

Narada's eyes lit up. 'That would be the solution to all of our problems. Where is she?'

Narayana shook his head, setting slightly atilt the jewelled crown on top of his soft curly black hair. 'I do not know. But there is one place she could be.'

Narayana and Narada travelled together to a corner of the Ksheera Sagara where the milky ocean met a sandy shore. This was no ordinary sand. Each grain was coloured a different hue, and together the grains created a mosaic of gem-like shimmers of pink, purple, red and orange. This matched the sky, which was similarly woven of different pastel hues. The soothing pink glow of the sand provided the only lighting. It was indescribably serene and still.

This was the site where most devas and devis were born or, more precisely, manifested in their present form. Usually, their arrivals were heralded with great fanfare, and there would be a bevy of devas and devis ready to greet them with the musical tumult of conch shells and kettle drums, throwing flowers and sandal paste in welcome. But it was as if this appearance had happened in secret.

Narayana inhaled sharply. He could tell she was here. He and Narada wandered the shore for many hours. The light never waxed or waned but remained a constant soft glow. They journeyed inland. After many yojanas of the sandy shore, which was as smooth and soft as silk beneath their feet, the shore gave way to a forest, which would eventually lead to the mountains.

It was in this forest grove that Narayana found Sati. Not exactly Sati, but he knew with a glance that this must be her incarnation. She was a young girl, dressed simply in white, hair streaming loose down her back. She looked confused, a little fearful, her eyes wide and pleading, a cluster of flowers clumped in her lap. Narada gasped in excitement, but Narayana shushed him before he could say anything.

Narayana knelt gently beside the girl and said, 'Hello. Do you remember who I am? Do you remember who you are?'

Usually, it was the utterance of a mantra that invoked all memories, all qualities, all powers back in the deva so they could ascend to their full state. Sati canted her head to the side. Regretfully, she shook her head.

Narayana said, 'You are S—'

Before he could complete her name, a bright red mass of fury launched into his chest and covered his mouth. Narayana sputtered as he sprawled on the ground, his wife firmly clasping her hand over his mouth, her eyes flashing anger at him.

Finally, Lakshmi removed her hand. The girl watched all of them wide-eyed.

Saraswati joined them, her pace leisurely, her countenance calm.

'What are you doing here?' Narayana asked warily.

Lakshmi's voice turned acerbic. 'You are not the only one who can tell when a devi is born.'

Narayana bit back a smile.

She continued, 'I will not let her suffer again, not this time. She would have a new life, a new opportunity.'

Saraswati agreed. 'She should be free, unbound to the past.'

Daksha's sacrifice. It was so vivid in all of their minds, though it had happened so long ago. The devastation wrought upon Sati the moment she had cast herself into the flames. Even Narayana worried that if it came to such a pass again, the universe might not survive this time. But Daksha was gone. And Shiva was in isolation. Didn't the world need Sati to return?

Saraswati read his mind. 'Perhaps. But it should be her choice.'

Narayana turned to the girl, who blinked slowly. There was such gentleness in her, such wisdom, such beauty, that he wanted to keep her with them in Devaloka, to nurture her into the devi she had been. He missed her. He missed the times when she would join forces with Shiva and him to destroy the demons and protect the mortals. He loved watching her in battle, fierce and fatally effective. But he, too, did not want to see her suffer.

Narayana softly whistled into the air and immediately, Garuda, the great eagle, appeared at their side. All of them—Narayana, Narada, Lakshmi, Saraswati, Sati—climbed onto his back. Garuda gently flapped his wings, bearing them aloft into the skies, and set off toward Mount Meru.

On the way, Narayana talked to the girl. He said, 'Because you are a devi, in fact, the greatest of all devis, you are free to choose your own life. Your form, your home, your family, your fate. Everything. We will protect you and make sure no harm befalls you.'

'But I do not know anything,' said the girl. 'How can I choose?'

Narayana smiled. 'When we arrive at Mount Meru, I will show you.'

Lakshmi and Saraswati remained silent. If they spoke too much to the girl, they would be overwhelmed with memories and longing for their sister. They would never be able to let her go. But they could not stop themselves from holding her hands.

They were careful when they landed on Mount Meru so as not to attract attention. They wanted to keep the girl disguised and hidden. She remembered nothing as she walked down the winding mountainous paths through the gardens she had frequented, the palaces of her friends and teachers, the bend in the road that led to the distant hut where she had met Shiva so long ago.

Finally, they approached a great library. Narayana evacuated the building with a snap of his fingers. Once they were satisfied that everyone had left, he ushered her inside.

She paused at the entrance. 'Who is that?' She pointed at an aged lion prowling the entrance, growling softly. He leapt towards her with sudden virility, as if he were once again a lion in his prime. He nuzzled her hand and licked it, gazing at her with adoring eyes.

'Dawon,' said Narayana softly. 'Do you want to take him with us?' He did not allow a note of hope to enter his voice.

For a long time, the girl ruffled the lion's mane. Something about him puzzled her, but she could not place it. Finally, she shook her head and turned away, walking into the library. As she turned away, Dawon's face froze into a rictus of desolation. His fur and mane iced into a million grey hairs. He slunk away, stooped and defeated.

Narayana took them into the chamber of maps. This was no ordinary room. As soon as they entered, the wooden platform on which they stood started spinning, and rows upon rows of pulsating planets arrayed themselves around the platform with the inky black night of space behind them. The others hung back as the young girl fearlessly walked to the edge of the platform. She watched carefully as different planets swung by her. Some were red and circled by many moons. Others were barren and desolate, cold to the touch. Some were dark and impenetrable. She picked only one. A blue planet speckled with white clouds. At her touch, the orb unfurled itself into a large globe, and she sent it spinning with a flick of her fingers. She touched the contours of the topography of continents and oceans until she landed on the icy peaks of the Himalayas.

She pointed to that blob of white and announced, 'There!'

Lakshmi leaned close to Narayana and whispered to her husband, 'Let her have a doting father. A simple and charmed life. Peaceful and undisturbed. Even if she has forgotten us, that is okay. So long as she is free.'

Narayana pronounced, '*Tathastu*. So be it.'

♋

Some time later, a girl was born to Himavan, the king of the Himalayas, and his wife Mena. She was the youngest of three daughters, known as Parvati. Himavan had a comfortable palace, but Parvati spent her days roaming the forests and green valleys that surrounded their home. She dipped her feet into the rivers and streams she crossed along the way. Sometimes she felt she was retracing footsteps from a lifetime ago.

Everything was quiet, still, stagnant. Everything was in wait. The trees had leaves, the valleys of her father's mountains were laden with green grass, but there was something missing, something nobody could any longer describe or identify as so many years had passed without flowers, without lush vegetation. Within her, she felt a hollow ache of longing for something or someone indescribable.

She talked to the wind, to the trees, to the blades of grass that bowed their heads to her every time she walked by. But there was one spot that did not respond to her. A steep path, covered by a thicket of trees, which led up from the forest floor to the snowy mountain passes high above. In her sixteen years wandering the forests, Parvati had never seen any creature, be it an insect or a bird or a mountain goat—let alone a person—climb or approach the path. Chills blossomed across her skin every time she passed by, simultaneously drawing her in and frightening her. She would look up at the mist-shrouded heights of the mountain, sometimes for hours.

That mountain haunted her dreams. Sometimes an invisible force pulled her up to the summit and as she reached, gusts of icy wind lashed against her and pushed her over the edge into a raging inferno of hot fire. She would wake up gasping as the flames suffocated her, as her skin was singed into ash. But whenever she closed her eyes, that mountain beckoned to her, gain and again.

One day, it started raining when she was in the forest. Rain was rare in those days. Perhaps once or twice a year a few desultory drops would fall, as if even they were reluctant to descend from the clouds into the suffering world below. But this was a storm, one Parvati had never seen before. It thrilled her, the power and force of it. For some time, she walked with her arms outstretched until she became drenched and cold. As she passed by that strange, steep mountain path, she noticed that the path was dry, as if the rain was too shy to trespass upon the walkway.

At first, Parvati only meant to seek shelter. That was why she set foot on that steep dirt track, or so she told herself. There was a coolness in the air, an invigorating breeze. She stood on that first step for a while. She hesitated, but a force arose within her that repelled any weakness or fear. She was stronger than that, she told herself. With a deep breath, she began climbing.

It was a strenuous trek, and she was someone who was accustomed to walking more than ten hours a day. The terrain was inhospitable. Rocks jutted out at difficult angles from each step, giving her no foothold. Every few minutes, a branch would swing out of nowhere, tiny thorns lacerating her cheeks. She felt the hissing of thousands of snakes as she made her way slowly up the mountain, almost warning her to keep away.

She craned her neck to look upwards. The sky was dark and grey, brewing with thunder and unspent storms, the tops of the trees knotting together protectively to keep the summit out of view. Something niggled at the back of her mind. The recollection of storm-swept seas, mountains of ice, gusting winds, whirlwinds of chaos—and in the midst of all that, two strong arms that held her in balance and kept her secure and safe. The brief reverie so overwhelmed her that she nearly lost her footing.

Who was that? What am I remembering? What or who am I climbing towards?

Distantly, she heard her mother calling out to her. 'Uma! Uma!' 'Do not go! Do not go!' That had become her mother's second name for her, she worried so much every time Parvati left the house.

Parvati blinked back tears, regretting how much pain she was causing her dear mother. Everything was crying out for her to leave, to go back home—her mother, the mountainside and all the creatures and living things in the forest. The air itself had become menacing and foreboding. Whatever it was that laid in wait at the end of the path clearly did not want her.

She had climbed for hours and was still less than halfway there. The darkness of night was falling. And yet, there was something stubborn in her that refused to go back. There was something that drew her to the mystery of what—or who—was waiting at the top of the mountain.

CHAPTER 14

'I did not expect you to be so easy to find,' said Narayana. He leaned against Garuda, who was blissfully napping after the journey from Vaikuntha to the Himalayas. He was snoring softly; softly for Garuda meant a deep rumbling that felt like an earthquake for many yojanas all around. Whenever Narayana was on his back or at his side, his sleep was joyous and peaceful. Those were the only times he could fully rest. Otherwise, he was a solitary bird, always on the hunt for snakes.

If a painter could have captured the sight, it would have been a most glorious portrait—the blue-hued Narayana reclining against the side of the giant eagle, gilded in the fading winter sunlight, surrounded by the snowy Himalayan peaks, talking to someone or something in a dark cave in front of him.

'Truly. I did not expect you to come to Earth, of all places. I searched for you a long time in Kailash, you know. It has really gone to pieces ever since you left. The *ganas*, who do not know what to do with themselves now, mostly fight with each other. I thought surely you would be at Kailash—there is nowhere more remote than there—if you truly wanted to be lost to the worlds. Yet here you are. An ordinary planet where mortals live. A place where anyone could find you.'

He glanced about and smiled. 'But, who would even know to look for you here? Maybe this is a good hiding spot for you after all.'

He rose to his feet and approached the cave entrance, ducking his head to peer inside. But he could see nothing. He just knew Shiva was there. Nothing could conceal Shiva from his perception. Even if he could not see him, he could feel that he was there.

He rubbed his jaw. 'Lakshmi would be most disturbed if she saw me like this, talking to thin air. She would think I've gone mad.' It was an odd feeling for him to miss anyone. After all, he was omnipotent, omnipresent, omniscient. The concept of lacking anything, needing anything outside himself, was inconceivable. But he missed the companionship of Shiva; they were two sides of the same coin. Only he could understand Shiva, and only Shiva could understand him.

It was a unique relationship. The *leela* of creation was not as enjoyable without their conversations, their bond. He thought he would try to annoy Shiva into consciousness.

'You know, without you doing your work, I am unable to go into meditation myself. I would like nothing more than to disappear into the midst of Ksheera Sagara, rest under the serpentine hoods of Shesha, and dream worlds into existence. Instead, I'm stuck hearing the pleas of this mortal, that rishi, meddling in the latest deva–asura dispute and basically trying to keep the universe from erupting into chaos and destruction. It is all rather tedious, I must say. You owe me a few million years of vacation time.'

My meditation is my work. He did not hear those words but imagined Shiva saying something like that, as he used to. Narayana smiled in fond remembrance. He offered a wave in the direction of the cave and approached Garuda to gently wake him and go back home.

But then the sound of rustling branches and leaves behind him caused him to turn around in surprise.

He was not alone after all.

♋

At first, Narayana did not recognise her. A sheen of sweat from the exertion of the arduous trek shone on her dark skin. She was slender, and her unscented, unadorned hair fell in a clumsily tied braid down her narrow back. She was dressed in rough-spun white cloth, plain and worn. She looked so very human.

But that pair of eyes—ah, Narayana would have recognised those eyes anywhere. Piercing, deep and fathomless pools of black that inexorably drew anyone in who looked upon her. And the way she held herself, with innate confidence and grace. There was an extraordinary pull to her, and even if he had not known her history, he would still impulsively have felt that the fate of the universe rested on her slender shoulders.

It had been a while since she had chosen to come to this world and start her new life. The wheels of karma and reincarnation ground slowly. When he had come to visit Shiva here, he had forgotten that she would be nearby. He wondered whether it was Shiva who had come first and drawn her here or whether it was Sati who had attracted him here by her presence.

Narayana quickly disguised himself as a poor woodcutter, with curly grey hair and beard, to avoid triggering any of her memories. She approached him curiously, panting lightly as she recovered her breath. Her eyebrows, fine and delicately arched, wrinkled at him.

'Who are you?' Growing up in the mountains under the indulgent parenting of Himavan and Mena, she never learned or had to bother with formality and etiquette.

He inclined his head politely. 'I am just a simple woodcutter about my daily work.'

She nodded. 'I am Parvati.'

Parvati. Sati. Even her new name rhymes.

Parvati's gaze swept over his face. 'I do not think you were the one I was looking for. Who were you talking to? I heard your voice before I got here.'

He fingered his beard. 'I am getting old and am not always right in the head. I thought someone was here, but it was only you. I was seeing things that do not exist.'

She marched over to him, her appraising stare frank and open. Narayana stepped back. It was as if she could see through his disguise. But luckily for him, he was not the object of her interest.

She tapped a long-tapered finger at the corner of her face. 'You seem quite lucid to me.' She looked around, her hair whipping this way and that in the wind. 'Oh, there must be someone else here. I knew I felt it.'

'Felt what?'

'Something cold and icy, like a storm, powerful and brewing. Something that drew me up here.'

Narayana's eyes darted to the cave. *Could it be true? Had she really felt the presence of Shiva?* But how could he explain a ghost to her, someone who had given up his physical form and body, who barely existed at all any more?

'There is no one else here.' He made his voice firm.

But, she followed the path of his eyes and knelt in front of the cave entrance. 'You're wrong,' she said in a satisfied tone. 'There is someone here. And I can see him.'

♋

Narayana was rarely surprised. This was one of those few times when he was caught off guard. He stood behind Sati and peered into the cave but could see nothing.

'What do you see, revered lady?' He kept up the appearance of being a simple woodcutter.

Her mouth had dropped open in awe. For some time, she did not speak. She just stared. She had never seen anyone like this and yet her eyes felt suddenly rested and replete, as if they had finally found what they had been searching for all her life, as if she were looking upon an old friend, an old lover. Her eyes drank him in, and the very sight of him nourished her, flooded her with strength and succour; it felt like she was coming alive for the first time.

She took long minutes to gaze upon his form. He sat in the lotus pose, his skin gleaming in the darkness of the cave like blue-grey ice. His eyes were closed, his face calm and peaceful, lips curled slightly upwards. From his body emanated a low hum, like a constant purring of Om. His hair was long and matted, a trickle of water wending its way through his tawny mane. His hands rested lightly on his lap, open and empty. Parvati watched those hands and absurdly wanted to place hers in his. A twinge of longing tore through her.

'Who is he?' she whispered. She lifted her little finger to point at him. As soon as she pointed at him, Narayana could also see Shiva sitting at the centre of the cave.

Parvati turned to look at the woodcutter.

Narayana squinted and pretended that it was the failing eyesight of an old man that had kept Shiva from his vision earlier. He remembered his promise. He would not tell Parvati that she had made Shiva visible, that there was this kind of intimate connection between them.

'Oh! Now I see him.' He cackled. 'This fellow? Well, he's a strange one. He sits like this, never bothering to eat or sleep. He may as well be a corpse.'

Narayana glanced at the darkening sky. 'Come now, it is getting late. Night will be falling soon. Let me see you home. It is not safe to be all alone in the forest as a young girl.'

Her gaze was back on Shiva. Her voice was placid. 'Oh, I am always alone in these woods. Nothing can hurt me. And I am not leaving.' Her tone became firm. 'I am not leaving him.'

'You can come back to visit him tomorrow. I am sure he will still be here. He has not moved in many years.'

She shook her head adamantly. 'I will not risk losing him; I will not leave his side even for a moment.' She sat in front of the cave, matching Shiva's posture. Her eyes never left him.

Narayana watched them both from the side. He rubbed his jaw. *This was always the problem with Shiva and Sati. They were extreme. Inseparable to a fault. Impractical.*

Completely absorbed in the intensity of their love for each other. Impossible to part, other than by death. He muttered under his breath. He had been hopeful, at first, that this new form of Sati would be able to bring Shiva back to the world. Now he feared that a new catastrophe was brewing. Shiva was too unpredictable. And she was too strong, too stubborn. He had hoped for a way to move beyond the tragedy that had befallen all of them at Daksha's yajna so long ago. He thought their reunion would restore order and harmony. But what if it just led their tragedy to repeat?

Narayana was not able to persuade Parvati to move even one inch from her seat. Instead, he accepted her request to visit her parents and assure them of her safety. In addition to their palace, her parents spent much of the time in a simple hut at the edge of the woods so that Himavan could watch over the mountains that were in his charge.

The smell of herbs and vegetables being smoked over a cheerfully burning fire drew Narayana to their wood cabin. The door was flung open as Himavan and Mena sat, anxiously looking out the door for their daughter.

At the sound of rustling leaves announcing Narayana's proximity, both Himavan and Mena jumped up and rushed to meet him. They did not often receive visitors. Wisps of greying black hair fell onto Mena's cheeks as she greeted him with a shy smile.

'You must be tired and hungry! Do come in and let us feed you, sir.'

Himavan looked the woodcutter up and down a few times before grunting in approval. He was a giant man whose towering form would have intimidated any ordinary woodcutter. His eyes narrowed upon Narayana's disguised form and looked past him suspiciously.

'Have you seen a girl on your way here? Have you seen my daughter?'

Narayana suggested that they talk inside. After the proper formalities were exchanged, Narayana explained the situation as delicately as he could.

Mena wrung her hands anxiously on her lap, her legs jiggling in apprehension. 'I have always worried about such a thing happening.' She threw a withering glance at her husband. 'You said not to trust the astrologer. But see, I was right.'

'What did the astrologer say?' Narayana asked curiously.

'Her birth was so strange. So many bright colours appeared in the sky the day she was born. Colours I have never seen before or since. You know how dark and drab our world is. Oh, shades of red, pink and yellow—colours I've only heard about in fanciful tales about times in the past when flowers used to bloom, when many different-coloured birds flew in the once dazzling blue skies. I saw all this when she was in my womb. Every time I felt her kick against my stomach, I would be covered with goosebumps, all the hairs on my body would thrill to know I was carrying such a powerful baby within me. When she was born, the sky shone like rubies.

'I did not know how to raise such a special child. I am a simple woman, after all. We do not get many visitors here. But soon after Parvati was born, I found a sadhu skilled at reading the stars roaming through these woods. I called him to look upon my daughter and tell me what I should do with her.' Her hazel almond-shaped eyes filled with tears. 'Oh, Parvati! Have I failed you after all?'

Narayana reached forward to pat her hand. She snatched her hand away and glared at him. He drew back hastily, remembering his guise as a poor woodcutter.

'I am sure she will be fine. She did not want you to worry. That is why she sent me here.'

Her eyes drifted away from him, staring out the open doorway of their hut. Darkness had fallen and from all around, there could be heard the hum of insects, distant howls and growls of night creatures mixing with the crackling of the hearth fire. Mena worried the edge of her thumb with her teeth, and Narayana could see she was imagining all the horrible fates that could befall her beloved daughter out in the dangerous world.

He wanted to say something ridiculous, such as that Shiva would never allow any harm to come to her. How preposterous that would have sounded, though.

Before he could say more, Mena continued, 'He told me that she did not belong here.'

Himavan snorted and grunted. 'How dare he say that? She is our daughter, after all.'

'He did not mean just us. He said she does not belong here, to this world. She belongs in worlds beyond our perception. That is what he said.'

Himavan warmed his hands over the fire, his jaw jutting out sullenly.

Mena whispered, 'I kept telling her, 'Don't go. Don't go. Uma, Uma.' It actually became her name. Uma. That was my pet name for her. But it did not work. She is gone.' She turned to her husband. 'Go, husband. Bring her back, please. We can keep her safe and well at home. I have a bad feeling. Who is this creature that has enchanted her? We do not know his intentions towards her. What if he hurts her?' Her fingers twisted in her lap. Clouds of curly hair fell out of her braid, covering the grief and anxiety etched onto her face.

'He will not hurt her,' Narayana assured her gently.

Her head jerked up. 'How do you know that? What do you know of him? Who are you, anyway? I have never seen you around here.'

He shrugged with a laugh. 'Ah, I'm just a simple woodcutter. I travel the woods and journey into different forests. I am never in a single place for very long. But I have seen this one for many years during my travels through here. He is always lost in meditation. He is a yogi, compassionate and kind. He would never harm a woman. Of that I'm sure.'

Mena looked beseechingly at her husband. 'I cannot just leave her like that. Please go bring back our daughter, my husband.'

Himavan got to his feet awkwardly. He had grown heavyset with the years, not as spry as he used to be. 'They call me Himavan, the king of the Himalayas. My whole life, I have tended to these mountains. I know how the mountains change with the seasons, all the creatures that roam through these woods. The first thing I think about when I wake up is these mountains, and they are the last thing I think about before I sleep, too. I belong to the mountains, but they do not belong to me. I am no king of these majestic stone castles. Just a guardian.

'Our daughter is bright and strong-willed. She is kind and gentle. She has lived her life in the wild forests of the Himalayas. She has made her choice. Who are we to control her destiny? I did not have visions when she was born, wife. But I did hear an *akash vani*, a voice speaking from the skies, that told me to let her be free, to let her be whatever she chose to be. And that has been my vow. No matter how much I worry for her, no matter how much I miss her, I will let her go. I will not own her as I do not own these mountains, which are my home. Let her go, Mena. Her fate is something bigger than you or I can see. We must make ourselves content with the days and years we had with her, without being greedy for more.'

Mena fell silent for some time. Her voice was hoarse with tears when she spoke again. 'So be it. Well, I am not such a fool to think you are a simple woodcutter, sir. You must be someone quite powerful, someone divine. Then it is up to you to keep her safe and to watch out for her.'

Narayana nodded solemnly, accepting the charge. As he passed Himavan, still standing at the doorway lost in thought, he placed a comforting hand on his shoulder. Narayana said, 'There was once a father who I wish had been as wise as you are, King. How much pain and loss would have been avoided had that been so. Because of your wisdom and the pure love you have for your daughter, something wonderful may happen. That which was once wronged may yet be restored.'

He gave up the disguise of the woodcutter, revealing himself as Narayana. Himavan and Mena fell to their knees in reverence and shock.

Narayana bowed his head to them gravely. 'The devas are in your debt.' And with that, he left.

♋

True to his word, Narayana watched over Parvati. He hid in the clouds to stay out of her sight. Wherever Narayana went, all the other celestials followed. The devas came, the *yakshas*, the *gandharvas*, the *kinnaras* and the rishis. They did not know the truth about Parvati's identity, but they were drawn subconsciously to her presence. They came for Narayana but stayed for her. In her, they found that sprite who had delighted Swarga, the kind devi who had smiled upon everybody, who had wandered happily through their forests, who had clapped in appreciation for their music and dancing, whose laughter had thrilled their very beings; the one of incomparable beauty and power before whom all of them had once knelt.

They never guessed that this simple human girl could have been that supreme goddess. But they were divine beings and saw with more than ordinary eyes. They saw that she was radiant as camphor, that her inner fire burned fierce. They saw how the clothes disintegrated and dissolved away from her body over the months and years that they watched her, that she did not bother dressing in anything other than simple woven bark. They saw that neither rain nor the scorching heat of the sun took her eyes off of Shiva. To protect her from the elements, they themselves sent clouds to cover the sun and caught the rain in their hands before it could touch her head. She was oblivious to their presence.

Sometimes, her parents came out of sheer concern over their daughter's well-being. They could not bear to stay for long. They could not stand the sight of her emaciated body, her once lustrous hair reddening and drying out from the sun. She had been soft as a flower, and now she was as hard and bare as bark. Her mother fretted over her, trying to brush away the hair falling into her eyes. Parvati rebuffed any attempts to touch her, to cover her in soft shawls, to feed her or pass water through her chapped lips.

'Won't she even eat?' Mena wailed to Himavan. 'At least, she used to eat fruit and drink water. Now she consumes nothing but air. She has become Aparna, *a-parna*, one who will not even eat a leaf.'

Himavan patted his wife's shoulder comfortingly. He said affectionately, 'You do have a talent for coming up with innovative names.'

She sniffled. 'What sad names they are! Uma— don't go. Aparna—one who won't eat even a leaf. What misfortunes have befallen my daughter!' She pointed a shaking hand at Shiva, blazing forth within the darkness of the cave. 'All for him? He is a rock. He is a statue that does not move. This bizarre creature with a snake around his neck, with water that trickles down his hair, covered in ash? This monster?'

Himavan clapped his hand over her mouth. 'Shhhh. Do not say such things, Mena. I'm not sure, but...this could be Mahadeva himself. Whole else could it be but Shiva? We dare not insult him. Let us go now. There is nothing we can do here.'

Mena swayed, weakened by concern. 'What has become of our daughter? Where is Narayana? He was supposed to look after her.'

Narayana appeared the next instant. 'I am here. Your daughter is safe. The wild beasts of the forest do not dare to trouble her. The heat of the sun, the fall of rain and snow—none of these touch her. She does not eat, but she is sustained through the power of her meditation.

The names by which you call her will one day be sacred. Beyond this, I cannot say more.'

Mena regarded him suspiciously, her hands akimbo. She nodded at Shiva. 'What about him? Will he hurt her?'

'Never,' vowed Narayana without a second thought.

She gritted her teeth. 'Well, isn't he hurting her now? Letting her starve herself for him? Letting her stay out here while he is safe in the cave? Shouldn't he protect her?'

'He is so immersed in his meditation that he is not even aware of her presence.'

Mena harrumphed. 'I do not know whether to wish for someone like that to even wake up. Who knows what he will do to my daughter then?'

Narayana promised softly, 'I will be here to protect her.'

'Hmmph! So even you do not trust his reaction to her. Even you agree this could all end in disaster.' Mena shook her head. 'Even you can offer no comfort to an old lady like me.'

Parvati's parents, now stooped and grey, walked away slowly, their tread heavy with anxiety and sorrow.

The mountain path, once so difficult and steep to traverse, had become well-trodden. Villagers thronged the mountainside to catch glimpses of Parvati. Stories spread far and wide about this young girl and her penance. They were fascinated by her intensity, focus and utter devotion.

They wanted to see a happy ending. Their lives had been colourless for so long. Laughter had disappeared from Earth. Love stories were not something they even dreamt of. Their existence was just survival. But there was something about Parvati that made them think there was more to the world and life than this. That there was place for beauty and love and play. They wanted to see her succeed, to know that they themselves could have some glimmer of an existence higher than daily subsistence.

But despite all the encouragement and hope of the devas and the mortals, nothing appeared to be working. Parvati sat so still that lizards and snakes climbed over her legs. She matched Shiva, penance for penance. But nothing roused him. It was like two statues facing off in stillness and silence.

Narayana and Brahma conferred. Narayana missed having these problem-solving conversations with Shiva. Brahma was not as much fun.

'We have to help her,' said Narayana.

Brahma sighed. 'I must reluctantly agree. If he persists like this much longer, we will be on our way to *pralaya* much too early.'

'We have to send him in.'

'Who?'

'You know very well who. The one we always call upon when we are in these difficult situations. The only one who can break the meditation of rishis and devas alike.'

'Isn't that her job?' Brahma pointed at Parvati from their vantage point high in the clouds.

Narayana chuckled. 'Yes. But she needs some expert help in making Shiva fall in love with her. It is time to bring him in.'

CHAPTER 15

'He will kill me, you know,' sighed the handsome young deva with the skin of a sea-green hue. Like all devas, he had many names—Manmatha, Kandarpa... but mostly he was known as Kamadeva, the deva of desire and love.

They were in Vaikuntha, sprawled on velvety red cushions as soft as clouds, sipping goblets of ruby-coloured fruit wine. Kamadeva was immediately suspicious when he had been given the place of honour, with Indra, Narayana and Brahma being most solicitous over his comfort, serving him the choicest slices of mango, his favourite fruit, and offering the wine to him first. If they were being nice to him, it meant that they were in deep trouble indeed.

He lifted his hand and his pet parrot came to perch on his wrist, squawking in warning to the others. It was all bark and no bite. Kamadeva had no real weapons, after all; his arsenal comprised just a sugarcane bow that shot floral arrows and the presence of Vasanta, the season of spring, with its fragrant breezes and delightful temperatures. Narayana and Brahma came to him only when they had no other option left, when they had to interrupt the meditation of rishis or asuras to restore balance.

But even Kamadeva had not expected that they would dare use him against Shiva. 'He already hates me. I have always been terrified of him, right from the start.'

Kamadeva had been born of Brahma for the express purpose of helping the process of procreation, to enchant couples into romance and love for the well-being of the world. Even the devas were susceptible to his powers. With the exception of Shiva.

Kamadeva had first tested his powers upon the devas when Sandhya—the most beautiful and chaste of women—was created. None had been immune to her charms and his spell, not even Brahma, who had fallen in love with his creation. Only Shiva had remained unmoved, and he had harshly condemned Brahma for harbouring inappropriate feelings for his progeny. Afterwards, before the birth of Sati, Kamadeva had tried again to shoot arrows in Shiva's direction, with no effect.

'Why now? Why approach me now?' Kamadeva was most reluctant.

Narayana interjected smoothly, 'There's a girl. She wants to win over Shiva. She cannot do so by herself. We want to help her.'

Indra chimed in, 'And also—'

Narayana cleared his throat. Indra and Narayana exchanged glances. There was something else afoot, another conflict in the air. But that would be a story for another time. Kamadeva groaned inwardly. If not today, he was sure to hear about this some other time, perhaps a few years or a few thousand years from now. Nothing was ever simple or straightforward in Devaloka.

He leaned his curly-haired head back on the pillows, gazing up at the brilliant blue sunlit sky. It was always beautiful here in Vaikuntha. His pet parrot nuzzled his shoulder comfortingly, sensing his distress.

'If it were anyone else, I would do it. You know I am always here to help. But not Shiva. He really will kill me. A death with no rebirth. I will be destroyed as if I never existed. I have felt so from the very beginning. That this Rudra will be the death of me.'

The other devas remained silent. *Is my death a price they have considered and deemed acceptable?* A delicate shiver trembled up his spine.

His wife, Rati, sat on the couch next to him. She held his hand in hers, which was already damp with the sweat of anxiety. Despite his general mood of terror, he could not help but smile at her. His beloved wife. Even though he was the deva of love and desire, there had never been another woman for him once they had united. From the beginning, she was his beloved. All the other couples that he had either united, reunited or broken up had only reinforced for him how special his relationship with Rati was. He squeezed her hand.

Rati settled against the cushions. He tightened his hand around the curve of her waist, pulling her into his side. She was voluptuous and petite, the bouncy curls of her hair framing the generous swell of her breasts. Just looking at her filled him with desire and passion.

Rati's large, expressive oval-shaped eyes gazed upon him, ignoring everyone else. She whispered, 'Husband, do you think you could help him? Not for the devas, not for the sake of Shiva, who could probably do with some more love in his life, but for my sister Sati?'

Such was Kamadeva's love for Rati that her sorrow sparked tears in his eyes. Rati, the daughter of Daksha Prajapati, the sister of Sati. How distraught Rati had been at Sati's death; how much she missed her still.

Kamadeva drew back and asked in a dry voice, 'You want me to help her husband unite with another woman?'

Rati rolled her eyes. 'Not when you put it like that. But she loved him so much. She would not want to see him in grief like this. She would want us to help him.'

Kamadeva sighed and leapt to his feet. 'So be it. I never can refuse you. Indra, yes, but not you.' He winked at Indra and walked to the door with his usual swagger. He turned back to look at the other devas coolly. 'I know what you think of me. How condescending you are to me. You think I am a joke, a trickster. Well, when Shiva kills me, which surely he will, you will see how much you need me. You will see that love and desire are the forces that keep the worlds spinning, that give life meaning and beauty. Not just for making babies and breaking vows. I will not do this for you. But I will do it for her—for Rati—and Sati.'

♋

Kamadeva waited until the devas were gone before he approached Parvati. With his hands, he shielded Parvati from the harsh glare of the sun. She turned her face to him questioningly. Her bones jutted out from her emaciated body. Her skin had bronzed and callused in the alternating sun and cold. Her eyes had become vacant and unfocused, her hair matted and rough.

Yet, as soon as Kamadeva saw her, he recognised her as Sati. He dropped to his knees and cried out, shedding tears of joy. Everyone else had missed it, other than Narayana and Sati's sisters. But his gaze was different from the other devas. He saw through the eyes of love. And he saw the intensity of love and devotion writ on her face, which he had only seen once before. Immediately, he knew it could only be Sati.

He choked out through his sobs, 'It's you! I cannot believe it's you! After all this time. Oh, it just has not been the same without you on Mount Me—'

'Who are you?' Parvati addressed him without looking at him.

He was crestfallen and his chin trembled when he realised she did not remember him at all. 'I am Kamadeva, Kamadeva...'

'Oh!' She hastily sketched a bow. 'I have never met a deva before.'

He glanced at her askance, peering up and all around, in all the corners where the devas and devis had been concealing themselves all along, in the darkness of the cave where Shiva shone as the most powerful of all the devas. Neither did the devas recognise her nor did she recognise those who surrounded her. What a strange situation!

'I have been sent to help you seduce him,' he explained.

'Why?'

He shrugged lazily. 'Oh, the fate of the universe depends on it, or else we are hurtling on our way to destruction and dissolution—you know, the usual reasons.' Parvati glanced at him quizzically. She could not imagine her love for the one in the cave could be so consequential. But she was willing to try anything.

'What will you do?'

He smiled. 'The usual,' he repeated. 'Shoot a few arrows. Spruce the place up a bit. Play some romantic music. And then, when he wakes up, he will see a beautiful woman.' Here, he wagged his eyebrows suggestively at Parvati. 'Voila, job done. World saved.'

Her lips curled downward dubiously. 'I do not think he's that kind of a deva. I do not think it will work.'

Kamadeva sighed dramatically. 'That I already know. I am sure he will kill me for it. But still, I will do it.'

'Why?'

'For you.' He gazed into her eyes, willing her to recognise him, to remember.

'Why for me?'

'Because we are friends.' The four words were full of affection and longing, nostalgia for long walks through the forests of Mount Meru, pointing out flowers to each other, drawing rainbows across the skies, competing to see whose would be the most colourful and stunning. He always lost to her. She was Shakti, after all. What he accomplished through schemes, tricks and spells, she achieved naturally and spontaneously. Love was what he conjured; love was what she was.

'I will fail, my dear, but you will not.'

Parvati's eyes floated back to Shiva. 'I have been trying for so long. So many years have passed already. I do not see how I could possibly succeed.' Yet nothing would persuade her to desist.

'Hmmph. Because you are doing it all wrong. You are trying to match him, ascetic to ascetic, penance for penance. Who can match the Adi Yogi in yoga?'

Her head fell. 'Is it so hopeless?'

He lifted her chin with a green finger. Tenderly, he said, 'Do not be him. Be you. When you remember who you are, that is when you will win.'

Her head tilted as she regarded him. 'Who am I?'

He dropped a soft kiss of benediction onto her forehead. 'The other devas often think I am useless. Well, I have my powers, too. I can grant boons, too. Here is my boon to you, my dear friend. At the moment you feel all is lost, you will find yourself, and in finding yourself, you will have found everything.'

♋

It was the most exciting event to have happened in all the worlds in ages. Kamadeva taking on Mahadeva himself. He waited for the best time when the season was most conducive, balmy yet pleasant. He brought out every weapon in his arsenal: the most enticing of musky fragrances, the most beautiful of flowers, which did not even bloom any more but had been safeguarded by him in his personal gardens ever since Sati's demise, the sweetest anklets, whose tinkling was enough to drive men mad. He brought Rati with him too. She reminded him of the truest and deepest meaning of love whenever he looked at her. He took his time, decorating the entrance to Shiva's cave, wreathing it with garlands and leaves.

The devas all assembled in great hope, thronging the Himalayas in carpets of clouds, blaring trumpets, banging on kettle drums and singing to the accompaniment of various stringed instruments. Parvati thought it a miracle that Shiva did not wake to that noise alone.

All the attention made Kamadeva even more apprehensive. Shiva did not like him, nor did he like crowds. This was not the way. You could not just cast spells and think it would result in love. How could Mahadeva be captured by flower arrows? The devas had badly misunderstood the situation.

He looked at Parvati. There was no nervousness, no hope, no anticipation, no fear writ on her moonlike face. She was perfectly calm. She had no expectation from her love for Shiva.

She is truly our only hope. I am just the joker in this play, catalysing her victory. But for her, that is a role I am willing to play.

Without further ado, he cast the spell. The air became laden with a sweetness almost cloying, a lingering scent of musk that nearly drove all the devas, *gandharvas*, *yakshas* and animals in the area mad with desire. For a moment, they even forgot about Shiva and the very reason they had come.

Only Parvati, Narayana, Kamadeva and Rati were immune. They held their breath, watching Shiva. There was a rippling across the surface of his skin, a wrinkling of his brow, a sniff through his nose—the only motion they had seen in him in the thousands of years he had sat there. A mix of dread and hope wrung Kamadeva's heart.

For a moment, Shiva's third eye opened. Less than a moment in fact. It happened faster than the blink of an eye. One moment Kamadeva stood before him, the bow from which he had shot the arrows of desire slung around his slim chest, and in the next, he was incinerated into a heap of ash. Rati screamed. She ran over to where her husband had been standing and stretched out her arms, but there

was not even a corpse for her to touch. She sobbed and
wailed in a grief so potent that it pierced the spell wrought
by her husband and woke the rest of the devas from their
stupor. They flocked to her in sympathy. Parvati watched
in horror as that beautiful woman's shoulders quaked. It
stirred something deep within her. Not just sympathy but
memory. Lovers separated by death, by incineration.

Sati, don't go.

Parvati shook herself. *Where did that come from? Who is
Sati? What am I remembering?*

She had never met Rati before but was about to walk
to her side to lend her whatever comfort she could when
a soft voice spoke behind her.

'Why are you troubled?'

Her mouth fell agape as she turned to see that Shiva
was talking to her. He appeared quite untroubled by the
clamour over the deva he had just killed, unruffled by
Rati's lament or the turmoil of the devas chattering and
clucking about her. His eyes were only on her, his third
eye again closed, a dimple of concern in the middle of his
smooth brow.

Shiva's eyes. She had never seen his eyes, never even
known his name or identity, so why did those tawny eyes,
drooping slightly at the corner, lazy and blissful at the
same time, as if the very universe were a joke that only
he understood, why did those eyes trigger such longing
within her? Longing for something she had once had
and lost so long ago? Why did she feel like she had seen
those eyes—knew every flick of light that danced within
them—that she had woken up to those eyes watching
over her fondly, those eyes that had traced her movements
with desire as she had danced for him?

She sucked in her breath, confused. He tilted his head. It seemed he did not know her either.

He repeated slowly, 'You look troubled. How can I help you?'

Parvati pointed at Rati, still wailing and beating her fists on the ground. 'I think she is the one who needs your help.'

Shiva snorted. 'I am asking you for the last time. What boon would you have of me?'

'You always give boons too easily.' The words slipped out before she could catch them. She frowned. *How did I know that about him?*

Shiva closed his eyes. He did not want to look at her any more. He did not know why he wanted to help her, why he could not bear to see her in distress. He was suspicious of Kamadeva. Maybe it was the lingering effects of his spell; maybe it was not enough to have destroyed and killed him. Better to close his eyes and retreat into meditation. He was a breath away from being lost to the worlds again when her voice roused him.

'Please bring him back to life.' Her voice was ragged. She herself did not know why it moved her so much to see this couple she did not know torn apart. She could have asked him for anything. She could have asked him to be her husband, for which she had been performing penance for so long. But she could not bear to see another couple broken in grief.

Shiva sighed. 'He is a pest. You could have asked anything from me and this is what you want?'

'Yes.' Apparently, Kamadeva had been her friend once. He had been kind to her. She could not see Rati's or any other woman's pain and not do everything in her power to help.

'So be it.' His voice grew faint. 'Not today, but one day. Someday, he will come back to life and take his physical form once more and be reunited with his wife.'

With those words, he withdrew again into meditation, turning as still and silent as stone.

Rati ran over to Parvati, covering her with kisses and hugging her tightly. 'Oh, bless you, Devi! Because of you, my husband will come back to me! I can wait forever for him. You have given me back my life. Oh, bless you, Devi!'

Parvati let herself be held by this wraithlike form. Narayana approached them, a sheen of sweat on his face, his eyes dark and brooding. He did not bother disguising himself this time. And Parvati had already deciphered who he was, who all the devas around her were, although she had not yet recognised herself. Darkness was falling around them, day giving way to night. Parvati felt bone-tired. The boon had been asked for and obtained, and once again Shiva had gone into meditation. She had never thought specifically what would happen when he woke to saw her. Some part of her had thought he would see her and that would be it—she would be his and he would be hers. Actually, she had never really thought about it all. She had seen him and had sat before him and never left. It was visceral, not something she had ever questioned or considered.

She got to her feet unsteadily. There had been years when she had stood on one foot under the blazing sun. There had been years when the ice from the mountains had melted into large glacial pools and she had stood neck-deep in that freezing water, visualising his face and body in front of her. There had been years when she lived on air and sunlight alone. Yet she had never been unsteady until now.

Narayana came to her side swiftly and caught hold of her arm. He sent Rati off with the other devas and held Parvati up until she regained her strength.

'I want to go home,' she whispered.

CHAPTER 16

Narayana walked Parvati home. They took breaks for her to rest. She had become weak and could barely take a few steps without her limbs shaking. Narayana had offered to simply fly her home on Garuda's back, but she wanted to use the power of her own body. She had grown accustomed to being frugal and self-reliant in all things.

As they stood in the midst of thick trees, bathed in silver moonlight, Parvati asked, 'Are you disappointed in my choice?'

'Disappointed? Why would I be disappointed?'

'Do you think I made the wrong choice? If I had asked him to marry me, do you think he would have said yes?'

'Oh, absolutely. He always keeps his word. He always delivers on his boons.'

Parvati blushed. 'I guess that must have been what you wanted all along. You hid, but I knew you were there with me from the beginning. You wanted him to wake up and stay awake. Kamadeva failed, and obviously, so have I.'

He turned to face her fully in the moonlight and smiled at her gently. 'To fail at something means to have had a specific objective in the first place. "After all, who knows, and who can say, whence it all came, and how creation happened? The devas themselves are later than creation, so who knows truly whence it has arisen? Whence all creation had its origin, the creator, whether he fashioned it or whether he did not, the creator, who surveys it all from the highest heaven, he knows—or maybe even he does not know."'

'That is from the Vedas.'

'Yes,' he nodded approvingly. 'If we do not even know where we came from, how can we know where we are going? I cannot tell you if Shiva should have gotten married for the first time, let alone a second time. I am just watching the cosmic game unfold.'

Parvati arched an eyebrow. 'You are hardly a passive bystander.'

He smiled. 'That is true. Yet, a long time ago, I had made a promise. One that I intend to keep. Parvati, you will always be free to be what you want to be and do what you want to do. You are not burdened by the plans and wishes of the devas. You are ever free.'

Parvati looked down at her hands, twisted into the faded bark skin dress she was wearing. Rati had cried so hard that her tears had softened the bark of her dress and almost dissolved it. She had worn it for the occasion of Kamadeva's effort to rouse Shiva. For many years, she had abandoned even dress, exposing herself naked to the elements. She had given up all modesty.

'I just could not stand to see Rati in pain,' Parvati said.

By then, they had reached Parvati's house.

'Of course, you could not. You could never see anyone else hurt. That is who you are, that is who you have always been.'

He could not keep back the emotion in his voice, as if he, too, was missing something or someone. Parvati saw the shadow of sadness pass through his eyes and wondered at it.

♋

Mena, afraid to let her daughter out of her arms for a single moment lest she ran away from home again, slept next to Parvati that night. Parvati, long accustomed to sleeping on the rough ground or not sleeping at all, chose to lay down on the bare floor. Mena lay next to her on a pile of warm blankets. Winter had brought a cold spell to their edge of the forest.

Mena's eyes became wide as saucers as she whispered excitedly to Parvati, 'Uma, that's SHIVA! Shiva! Can you imagine? Mahadeva himself! Why did you never tell us that?'

'I did not know. I knew he was special, of course. But I did not know who he was. And I did not care.'

Mena squeezed her hand. 'I never recognised him either. There was a time when the devas used to wander among us on Earth and we knew them as our own family. Long, long ago, Shiva and Sati used to travel through the Himalayas and would meet with people and bless them, eating with them, celebrating festivals with them. Now those days are gone.'

'Sati.' *Sati, do not go.* Again, she shook off those words.

Mena's voice grew firm. 'Yes. Sati. His only wife. His only love. I understand why you are...fascinated by him. But child, you know, you are only human. And he is Mahadeva.'

'I know.' She told herself she had never expected anything of him.

Mena squeezed her elbow, 'I mean, he is SHIVA. What if it had worked? What if he had married you? He would be my son-in-law! How could I have Mahadeva as my son-in-law? How could I invite him to this house? I have never in my life had a snake in my house. I am not about to start now!'

'He is not like that,' Parvati protested indignantly. 'He would be gentle and kind to you.' In the recesses of her memory, flashes of a long-ago wedding flickered in and out. A handsome bridegroom, solicitous of her mother, bowing before her with a smile. A different mother, but the same Shiva. Her head began to hurt and she shook it once again.

Mena harrumphed. 'In any case, it is best you have come back home. This is where you belong, Parvati.'

♋

For some time, she really did try. She stopped going into the forest and stayed at home with her mother, helping with the cooking. She still could not bring herself to eat anything other than fruit and milk. But she liked to feed her parents and the increasing number of visitors who thronged their home from all over to see her. They thought she was a devi, that she had some secret powers, that she could bless them.

She tried to disabuse them of this notion, but the more she protested the more convinced they were that she really was a devi.

She tried to enjoy the comforts of living at home, of being part of a family. But every moment of every day her thoughts were on that cold mountainside, on the grey ash-smeared body of Shiva inside the cave, the feeling of the hard earth beneath her thighs as she meditated with him in the silence of the night. She missed him. She missed herself, as she had been on that mountain.

This is not all that I am. I am more than this.

Kamadeva's words came back to her. *In finding yourself, you will find everything else.*

Her breath, her heart, her mind—they only knew one name. Shiva. Shiva. Shiva. As if she were the one who had given him that name.

One night, after the day's work had ended and her father had gone to sleep, Parvati stood next to her mother, cleaning the household utensils and vessels to be used again in the morning.

'Ma—'

'Do not tell me,' Mena said sharply. 'I already know. I know what it is to run away for love. A long time ago, my parents did not want me to marry your father. They did not think being the king of the mountains was illustrious enough a position. I did not care. We got married in the *gandharva* fashion, for love, and came away here.'

Parvati hugged her from behind, gently stroking the grey hair from her eyes. 'Ma, do not tell me not to go away.'

Mena stood stiffly in her embrace for some time. Then, with a sigh, she relented and softened her body, clasping Parvati to her. 'Fine, child. Go, but come back. Come back with Shiva. Come back with my son-in-law.'

She went to him at midnight on Amavasya, when there was no light in the sky. When even the stars had hidden behind the clouds. Narayana was not there when she came. None of the devas was. She and Shiva were alone.

She did not sit for meditation this time. Kamadeva had been right. She could never match him in penance. *Find yourself.* She stepped into the cave. It was dark and bare. Dust and dirt covered the cold stone. *It should be clean. He should be sitting in a clean, comfortable place.* At that thought, immediately the dust and dirt cleared. Parvati frowned. *How had that happened?* There was no deva here to help her. It could only have come from her. She looked at her hands. *What kind of power lay in them?*

She knelt in front of Shiva. His eyes were hooded, his mouth in a half-smile. Maybe he was happier this way. Maybe she should let him go, let him be like this, undisturbed, lost and content in his thoughts. *I will look at him just one last time and leave.* She let her eyes savour the sight of him. Each sinew and curve of muscle in his body, the tawny hair, the broad chest. Reluctantly, she rose to her feet and walked backwards out of the cave.

Blinking away tears, she whispered, 'Be well.'

She was about to turn away when the thought came unbidden to her—*I wish the cave could be prettier somehow. I wish it could be decorated with flowers. I wish it were beautiful for him.*

A teacher's voice from long ago rang in her ears, reminding her about balance and harmony, about complementary halves of a whole. About balancing beauty with strength. About light and darkness. A soft pink orb hovering above her palm, a world that she had created.

What was beauty? She wondered to herself. She had never known beauty, never seen it. It had been shorn from this world, from all the worlds, long ago. *What was a flower?* Had she ever seen a flower, other than the ones that shot from Kamadeva's arrows, incinerated along with him as soon as Shiva had opened his third eye.

She suddenly longed to see beauty, to see a flower. An upswelling began within her. Long dormant forces and energies started to awaken and tingle her blood. No sooner had she thought of flowers than the cave became carpeted with them. Red, pink, yellow, blue, green, violet, colours she had never seen before, colours she did not even know existed. She took petals in between her fingers, luxuriating in the sensation of soft, smooth silkiness.

Pink fingers began to paint dawn into the sky. But the dawn was missing something. *There should be birdsong,* thought Parvati, though she had never heard a bird sing in her life. Within a moment, the skies filled with gaily coloured birds, chirping and singing to each other excitedly. Life pushed upward through the barren ground, colouring the plains with green grasses and lush, verdant vegetation, trees bursting with fruits and flowers and all hues of leaves. For hours, Parvati summoned life back into the universe. It burst like watercolour against a blank canvas. The world had fragrance again, the smell of delicate flowers, of fertile soil, of nourishing rain moistening the damp land.

Parvati revelled in it, but still, Shiva was impervious. There was something else, something she had forgotten. In all this time, she had never called him by name. She had meditated on his name; she had recited it in the silence of her heart. But she had not dared to call out to him. She did so now, impelled by longing and desire she could no longer suppress.

'Shiva.'

At the sound of those two simple syllables, memories flooded her. The first time she had called him Shiva, on the Night of Rudra, how he had smiled at her.

Find yourself, and in that, you will find everything else.

The night of her *vahana* ceremony, when he had put the moon in her hair. Her eyes fell closed. Once she had not known who she was. He had shown her all her forms, all her names, all her powers. He had married her on a starry night on another mountainside when she had belonged to a different family. Her father. The yajna. Shiva's last words to her.

Sati, do not go.

It all came back to her.

Memories. Longing. Most of all—love.

Love is what I conjure; love is what you are.

It burst out of her like a raging fire that would consume all the worlds. Love. Not just her love for Shiva, but the cosmic love which they generated together, the love that sustained the worlds, that contained within it all the force and power in the universe, the source of love from which sprang every form of love—that between mother and child, brothers, lovers, friends. It left her spent.

She sagged against the wall of the cave, her face covered with tears and sweat. All the worlds had come back to life, but still, Shiva sat immobile as a statue.

'Shiva,' she said once more. *Shiva, I have come back. Will you not accept me?*

Then, from the skies, from the distant heavens far above, descended a small white flower, a flower of such intricate design and beauty that only two had ever been able to fashion it—a white flower that a young devi had once seen in the distant corner of Mount Meru, a flower growing on a tree by an abandoned hut, which Shiva had once tenderly placed into her hair.

That flower drifted down from the skies and floated past Parvati's head, landing delicately on Shiva's nose. Who can say where it came from? Had it come from the power of Parvati's creation? Or Shiva's meditation? Or from some source which even the devas could not know?

At the tickle of the flower against his nose, at that scent, that unique scent that could only be traced back to this singular flower, Shiva opened his eyes to see his wife standing before him. For the first time in so many millions of years, Shiva smiled.

'Sati.'

His voice was as warm as the sacrificial fire of yajna. His eyes lit up in indescribable joy. Sati began collapsing to the ground out of sheer exhaustion, but Shiva caught her up in his embrace, cradling her against him. He carried her outside the cave. It was time to go back home.

On the planet of Earth, amid the snowy peaks of the Himalayas, there is a high mountain valley, covered by endless groves of pine trees. The temperature in that valley is always a little cool, the gentle breeze wafting through the thin air scented with pine and other vegetation. There is a serenity there that can hardly be found in any of the many other worlds that populate this universe.

It was in this valley that Shiva and Parvati were married. Shiva had chosen the site. He wanted a place that was remote, inconspicuous, unfrequented by immortals and mortals alike. It was a place he had romped through in his sojourns through the Himalayas. And, Parvati, too, had spent many a pleasant afternoon napping among the pine trees. So many days they had spent in this valley, separately, and now it would be the place where they restarted their life as a couple.

They wanted to avoid the crowds that normally plagued the wedding of any deva or devi, but it was the wedding of Mahadeva and Shakti, after all, so there was no stopping the throngs of devas, *gandharvas*, apsaras, rishis and, of course, the *ganas*. But Shiva must have had a stern word with the *ganas*, as they were scrupulously well-behaved and looked as if they had even bathed that very day.

Mena, as excited as she was for the wedding of her daughter to the greatest of the devas, to see her daughter finally happy and healthy, was intimidated by the fierce manner and appearance of Shiva. To soothe her, Shiva transformed his appearance. His hair was smoothed into a dark luxuriant mane of black tresses, as velvety and deep as night. He kept his tiger skin wrap, but for once he left the ash off his body. He shone like a crystal. His face was unadorned and young and beautiful, his eyes gleaming with ardour for his wife-to-be, his lips curved in a tender, beneficent smile to put all those who saw him at ease.

He gracefully bowed down to Mena before the ceremony began. He was so solicitous and affectionate as a son-in-law—one who had been born to no mother—that she looked at him through a veil of tears and murmured her blessings.

It was a wedding like none that had ever come before it and none that would ever come after. Brahma himself was the officiating *purohit*. Narayana presided over all. He became so absorbed through the ceremony, so devoted to the marriage between Shiva and Parvati, that the site of the ceremony became forever after known as Triyuginarayan, the place where Narayana himself is present during all three *yugas*.

Mountainous masses of rice, beaten rice, jaggery and sweets were heaped for the pleasure of the devas, *yakshas*, *gandharvas*, *kinnaras*, *siddhas*, apsaras and rishis. Himavan constructed huge tanks to store the ghee, yoghurt and barley cakes. Fountains flowed with nectar and sugarcane juice. Spicy pickles were prepared especially for the *ganas*.

The mountains themselves came to witness the wedding. Even Kailash came. The sacred rivers came, too, chief among them being Ganga. So many tents had been pitched, so many flags strung up, that the sunlight was crowded out of the sky. Vishwakarma constructed mansions for Narayana, Brahma, Indra and all the devas, just for the wedding festivities.

The sacrificial fire that burned that evening, the fire around which Shiva and Parvati circumambulated to solemnise their marriage, was peculiar. Usually, it was

Agni who personified fire, who was the medium through which offerings were made and conveyed to the devas and the ancestors. Yet, in this fire, Agni had stepped away. It was too powerful a union, too sacred a rite, for him to participate. Instead, it was Shiva and Parvati who combined and poured forth their energies into a golden, sandal-scented, incandescent fire.

It was around this fire that they took their first steps as bride and groom. This fire was so special, so powerful, that for aeons to come, those who came to Triyuginarayan could see and worship that very same fire. It was a fire that through the end of time would never go out.

Many hours passed after the ceremony had ended, and still, the devas and *gandharvas* were celebrating festively with goblets of fruit juices and intoxicants and platters of rich food, which kept appearing from the celestial kitchens. The night was starry and beautiful, the moon out in full glory basking in joy upon the special occasion.

Yet, Shiva and Parvati wanted nothing more than to go home to Kailash. Finally, Shiva took Parvati's hand and drew her to his side.

'Honestly, I do not think anyone will notice if we leave.'

Parvati looked up at him with sparkling eyes. 'Even if they do, would you care?'

'I cannot wait a moment more.'

As he led her away from the crowds, intent on going back to their cave in Kailash, Parvati teased him. 'I do not think you missed me at all. You were so deep in meditation you did not even notice I was gone.'

Shiva chuckled. 'I know you are fishing for me to say something sentimental, my dear wife.'

'It is the day of our wedding after all. You could say one sweet thing to me.'

He came to a standstill, twining her fingers into his. 'I missed you so much that once I visited a river, the Kalindi. Even bathing in the river reminded me of you. I was so desolate without you that the colour of the water changed to black and has remained black ever since.' He pulled on her ear affectionately. 'Is that sentimental enough, wife?'

She nodded, her heart too full for words.

♋

Shiva and Parvati delighted in their reunion for a few million years. It took repeated, polite throat-clearing from Narayana and Lakshmi, as well as a few impatient growls from Nandi, before they could be persuaded to emerge from their cave on Kailash, yawning and stretching.

As they sat to drink a special brew of herbal tea that only Parvati knew how to make from a mix of rare herbs she used to collect, Nandi plopped down on Shiva's lap and stared the others down with an imperious, possessive gaze.

Before Parvati could ask about Dawon, her lion, Nandi muttered, 'He is fine. I have been watching over him. He will be here soon. He has been waiting like I have.'

Parvati stretched out her hand to pet Nandi's back. How loyal and patient were their *vahanas*; how much they must have suffered waiting for them all this time. The devas themselves were immune to the vicissitudes of time. What felt interminable to others was a mere blink of an eye for them. It made existence rest lightly on their shoulders.

Shiva looked at Narayana through half-lidded, sleepy eyes. 'So, did we miss anything?'

Narayana complained, 'Both of you left behind quite a mess. I've had to run here and there to keep the universe in working order. I believe I deserve a vacation now.'

Lakshmi squeezed her sister's hand. 'Do not mind him. It's not all bad. Now the two of you are more popular than ever before. The most romantic couple ever to grace Devaloka. Do you know, Parvati, there are now millions of women who are fasting to get a husband like Shiva? Not that anyone can match what you did, of course.' A note of pride and admiration entered her voice.

Shiva grunted. 'To get a husband like me? What nonsense. If anything, the men should fast to get a wife like Parvati. Why would anyone want to have a husband like me? They should die to get a wife like mine.'

Lakshmi turned to Narayana. 'Why do you never say such things to me? That is why he is so popular now, you know.'

Shiva said wistfully, 'It was so much nicer when everyone feared me.'

Narayana sighed. 'You will regret saying such cruel things to me, wife, when I am far away in Ksheera Sagara.'

Parvati asked, 'Are you leaving?'

He nodded. 'I have been much too active for the last many millions of years. It is time I go back to cultivating my *tapas* and withdraw for some time.'

Narayana's meditation differed from Shiva's. Shiva's was of the nature of *pralaya*, the withdrawal of the cosmos into itself, dissolution and destruction. Narayana slept on the serpentine bed of Ananta in the depths of the milky ocean and dreamt worlds into existence. Through his breaths, all the worlds were sustained.

Lakshmi's face darkened. She was able to spend time with Narayana when he was in Ksheera Sagara, but it was not the same as their time in Vaikuntha.

Parvati stroked her hair. 'Don't worry. We'll get to spend a lot of time together while he's away.'

'Will we?'

'Of course. I will come to Mount Meru often. We'll be together like the old days.'

Lakshmi smiled at her slyly. 'In the old days, you weren't married.'

Parvati looked down at her hands. 'Saraswati was right, you know. I was trying to avoid a conflict that was inevitable. I belong here, but I also belong to Mount Meru. We each have different roles and identities. The greatest love is the one that does not make you choose between them but accepts all of them. Shiva has shown me all the different names and forms and roles I have, and I have brought out new ones in him. I belong here with him, but I also belong with you and Saraswati, with my teachers and friends back home.'

Later that night, Shiva and Parvati were taking an evening flight across the galaxies on Nandi's back. Parvati snuggled against Shiva's broad chest. 'This is not so bad, is it?'

'What is not so bad?' He whispered into her hair.

'Being married. Being a householder.'

'Hmmm.' He nuzzled the back of her neck with a tender kiss. 'It is nice. I like having a wife after all.' Then in a firm voice, he added as an afterthought, 'But no children.'

PART III

THE CHILDREN

CHAPTER 17

'I think we have a child,' Parvati said to Shiva one morning.

They were walking through the narrow footpaths of Kashi. The fragrance of incense wafted out of the doorways, where the glimmering lights of *aarti* shimmered and bells tinkled. They had disguised themselves as an elderly couple. If recognised, they would have been inundated with showers of flowers and sweets. They did not want to hassle the good citizens of the city. They enjoyed the serene ambience of Kashi as commoners.

Shiva burst out laughing, attracting the attention of nearby pedestrians who stared at them curiously. They could disguise their looks, but Shiva's laugh was unique, like the rumbling of a volcano.

'Wife, I know I am often oblivious, but I think I would have noticed if we had a child running around.'

He made a show of looking around them, checking under the street carts filled with fried *pooris* and coconuts to see if there was a toddler there. Parvati swatted his arm in mock irritation.

'I am a woman. Women know these things. It's a maternal sense. I feel it in my bones. I feel a piece of me is alive and somewhere in this universe. I feel the pangs of separation from my child. The child is real, Shiva.' She whispered his name. The people of Kashi were mad for Shiva and would have pounced on him if they knew he was there.

Shiva looked at her askance. 'Were you pregnant and I did not notice? Am I so careless a husband?'

Parvati tugged on her braid, thinner and grey in her assumed form. 'You know the ways of the devas are mysterious. You know there are many ways for children to be born. Not just the obvious. Particularly if we are involved. We may have had a child born out of meditation, out of the bliss of our union, without even knowing it.'

'Hmm. Okay, I shall have the *ganas* search high and low for him or her. If we truly have a child, it would be impossible for them to remain hidden.'

Parvati swallowed hard. 'Are you unhappy about the possibility?' She remembered his words when they had reunited—no children.

Shiva laughed. 'I was just teasing you. Whatever happens, I am happy.'

Indeed, as Shiva had predicted, it did not take very long to find him.

Who could hide the brilliance of the son of Shiva and Parvati from the world? The mountains could not bear his weight. The oceans could not bear the fiery energy burning within him. The sun hid in the west, overwhelmed by his effulgence. It was not difficult to find him at all.

Nandi was the one to approach him. He was a six-headed boy, as golden in hue as his mother in her form as Gauri. In one hand, he held a spear. In the other, he hugged a peacock that stood nearly as tall as him. The *ganas* found him in a grove of reeds near the Ganga. He was encircled by a group of six women, who gazed upon him dotingly.

Nandi recognised him immediately. Who else could this beautiful boy be but the son of Shiva and Parvati? Nandi trotted to his side, bowing his head respectfully. The boy watched him with bright, curious eyes. The women surrounded him protectively.

Nandi announced in a grave tone, 'I am Nandikesvara, the chief of the *ganas*. I have been sent by Shiva and Parvati to bring you home to Kailash. You are their child.'

The boy cocked one of his heads at him. 'Hello, Nandi.'

Nandi scuffed the ground with his toe in a friendly gesture. 'What is your name?'

With his small hands, the boy indicated the six women surrounding him. 'These are my mothers who have watched over me my entire life. They are the wives of great rishis. They are the *krrtikas*. From them, I take my name, Karthik.'

And so was the son of Shiva and Parvati called Karthik. An ageless child, he was not surprised by the appearance of Nandi. Nor did he hesitate to take leave of his mothers, comforting them with hugs and words of solace as he mounted the chariot crafted especially for him by Parvati. His foster mothers beat their chests and wailed at the separation. From the skies, he blew them a kiss.

As they flew on the chariot wrought of ornate silver and lined with silken cushions, Karthik looked at Nandi. 'Do you know how I was born?'

Karthik raised his eyebrow in an imperious way that reminded Nandi of Shiva.

Nandi squirmed. 'Erm...well, it's a mystery, actually. Mata Parvati...she just sensed your presence. She knew you were somewhere out here. We just don't know...umm, that is to say, I am not clear on how you were born?'

Karthik's gaze intensified upon Nandi's face. His eyes were light hazel, sparkling with wit. When he became serious, they darkened into pools of black kohl. His voice was flat. 'You may not know how I was born. But I know why I was born. That I have known since the day I was born.'

Nandi was fascinated. 'Really? What is the reason?' His voice dropped to a whisper as he leaned forward in excitement.

'I was born to kill. The devas wanted me to be born for that purpose, so that is what happened. Tarakasura, the demon, has been terrorising them for ages. Shiva and my mother—they were missing in action, as it were, while Shiva went into meditation and Parvati tried to win him over. Then they reunited and left for Kailash. They have been away from the worlds for too long, letting Tarakasura run wild and free. The devas grew desperate.'

Something tickled at the back of Nandi's mind. A distant memory. He searched through his memories until it dawned upon him. He had heard how Kamadeva had been sent by the devas to interrupt Shiva's meditation and how his master had killed Kamadeva. In the beginning, he had thought it was out of sympathy for Parvati that they wanted to help her win his love. But he had always been suspicious there was more to it, that there was more urgency around why they wanted Shiva to awake. The ways of the devas were complex and cryptic. There was always a game afoot. Now it made sense.

Karthik continued in a smooth tone. 'In the absence of my father, they had to rely upon me, the son of Shiva. I was deemed the only one who could defeat Tarakasura. And thus, I was born.'

Nandi was puzzled. 'Without your parents' consent? Wouldn't they have to, erm, conceive and give birth to you?'

Karthik looked out of the open sides of the chariot, over the oceans swiftly passing under their feet. 'I am just a child. What would I know of such things?'

Nandi remembered, though, the long reunion of Shiva and Parvati when they had returned to Kailash. How the devas had kept coming and trying to interrupt their privacy. Somehow, someway, out of the passion and intensity of that intercourse, this boy had emerged, this son they had not even known they had created. And the devas had whisked him away to carry out the mission they had foisted onto his young shoulders.

'I see,' said Nandi. Something about the set of the young boy's shoulders, the rigid way in which he held himself, his unflappable personality, disturbed Nandi. He had lived with six mothers, knowing one day he would be taken away and that he had been born only to kill another. He had not even known the love of his birth parents. His existence was secret, his origins mysterious. It was a terrible burden to put on one so young. Nandi could not help looking at him pityingly.

Karthik sensed it, and his back stiffened.

'Are we there yet?' he asked in a petulant voice.

At that, Nandi smiled with relief. The child was still there in him yet.

♋

Of course, the son of Shiva and Parvati was greeted with great fanfare. There was much garlanding and gifting by all the devas, showers of flowers by the *gandharvas*, singing and dancing by apsaras, and the festivities went on for a long time. But Shiva and Parvati shooed everyone away after some time, impatient to spend time with their child. Well, Shiva was impatient. Parvati had become suddenly shy and withdrawn, lurking in the background.

After everyone had left, Shiva sat on the floor with Karthik. Throughout the day, Karthik had been very formal and polite, so articulate in his expression. His intelligence was quick and piercing. He accepted the obeisance paid to him with a gravitas far beyond his tender years. Shiva was worried that he had grown up too soon.

He wondered how to make his son laugh. He had never played with a child before. He sent his *ganas* in all directions with orders to find and bring back for Karthik the most entertaining toys ever known to exist. The *ganas* searched far and wide, breaking into homes to fetch toys, apologetically reconstructing houses and soothing terrified homeowners on their way back. Soon, Karthik was surrounded by thousands of glittering toys and dolls. But he showed interest in none of them.

This vexed Shiva. A displeased frown on his face was enough to terrify even Narayana and Brahma. But Karthik was unperturbed.

Shiva said sternly, 'You must choose at least one toy to play with. For at least one hour. That's an order.'

Karthik nodded. Shiva was his father, after all, so he had to obey. He did not spare a glance for any of the toys, though. Instead, he walked over to Shiva and knelt on the ground in front of him. He pointed at Vasuki, the snake wound around Shiva's neck. 'That. I want to play with that.'

Shiva grinned in delight. Karthik was truly his son. He nodded and took Karthik onto his lap. Karthik chuckled happily and played with Vasuki, petting him excitedly with his hands and teasing him affectionately. Shiva burst out laughing at Karthik's antics and kept watching his son, kissing his forehead repeatedly, his throat so choked with emotion that he was unable to speak.

His eyes searched the room for Parvati, wanting to share this moment with her. She was hiding in the shadows, tears streaming down her face as she watched the entire scene. She was bereft at the thought of how much time, how many similar scenes she had missed out on with her son, that she had been separated from him without even knowing it. She had been a mother to the universe for as long as she could remember. But she had not been able to be a mother to her own son. Shiva beckoned to her to join them. Hesitantly, she sat next to them on the floor, leaning into Shiva's shoulder, where Karthik sat tucked into the strongly muscled curve of his father's arm.

Karthik saw the tears falling from his mother's eyes. He reached out a chubby hand to pick up the corner of her gauzy pink pallu and used it to wipe her cheek. That little gesture broke the dam of feeling within Parvati and she began laughing and crying at the same time, seizing him from Shiva's arms and hugging him to her chest. He snuggled contentedly into her embrace.

Later, she would ask him about his other mothers, who they were, how they had taken care of him, where they were. Then, she would visit them and bow to them. It was not for her to bless them when they were the ones who had blessed her. She was Jagadamba, mother of the universe, to whom all bowed, but she was humbled by them. Later, she would scold the devas for their interference.

But today all that mattered was that they were all together as one family. Anyone looking upon the tableau of that divine, loving family would have been enchanted. Anyone would have thought they would be happy together forever—a close-knit family destined to be together eternally. They would have been wrong.

CHAPTER 18

One day, Parvati was visiting Lakshmi in Vaikuntha. They were strolling through Lakshmi's private gardens. The walking paths were paved with smooth gems, warm and soothing beneath their feet. Bees swarmed around their faces and necks, drawn to the jasmine and marigold garlands they wore. Flowering bushes stood as tall as their heads, creating a pleasant labyrinth through which they walked, concealed from the view of the winged *gandharvas* who sat in the towering trees nearby, humming and singing their musical compositions.

'How is Karthik?' Lakshmi squeezed Parvati's hand.

Parvati shook her head. 'Oh, one would hardly think he is a child any more. Do you know that he has already moved out to his own mansion? Off to war already, before I've even had a chance to get to know him.'

Lakshmi smiled sympathetically. 'Well, it is a great honour, you know, to be appointed as the commander of all the devas.'

'Hmmph. Sometimes I feel he was never mine at all. He was born to carry out the mission of the devas, to destroy a demon. I feel he does not belong to me.' An unexpected bitterness roughened her voice.

'You're his mother, Parvati!' Lakshmi was alarmed by Parvati's mood.

'Am I? I think he considers those six *krrtika* women—who raised him, who fed him the milk of their breasts, who watched over him from birth to boyhood—his mothers. All this time he was living by himself in the middle of nowhere, and I was... I was unaware. How could I have been separated from my son without even knowing it?'

Lakshmi tugged on Parvati's hand, pulling her down to sit next to her on a bench so that they could rest and talk properly. 'What exactly happened?' Karthik's origins were mysterious. Even the devas were not certain where he had come from, how he had been born.

Parvati fidgeted with her emerald-green sari. She was resplendent today in a new diamond-studded sari woven by her mother, Mena, on her last visit back to the Himalayas. She had captured the verdant green of the foliage in the forests where Parvati had once roamed as a girl. The diamond studs were shaped into the tiny animals and critters who had sat with her as she had gone through her extraordinary penance. She had decided to dress up to visit her sister today. It was useless dressing up for Shiva since he hardly noticed whether she was dressed or naked.

'When Shiva and I came back to Kailash and were—' she cleared her throat delicately. 'Reuniting, the devas came and interrupted us at one point. They created such a ruckus that we had to get up and see what they wanted. They were crying out for us to give them a son who could defeat Tarakasura. I was so angry

at their interruption that I banished them on the spot.
I even cursed them that none of them would ever have a
child. While we were getting rid of them, part of Shiva's
seed fell to the ground. It's a long story, but eventually, it
found its way to the banks of the Ganga and transformed
into Karthik.'

Lakshmi was intrigued. 'Such a bizarre conception
and childbirth could only happen to you and Shiva!'

Parvati wrung her hands in her sari, dampening the
flimsy fabric with sweat. 'True. Why is it, Lakshmi, that
we are the only ones who have a child anyway? I never
thought about having children before. None of us has
them. You and Narayana never had a child—'

'That's kind of true. But when we descend to Earth in
human form as our avatars, we have children—like when
he was Rama and I was Sita or when he was Krishna and
I was Rukmini. In Devaloka, I suppose—well, there must
be some kind of *moha* or desire from which children are
born, right? Here we are all so content and fulfilled that
we never even think of having children.'

Parvati smiled sadly. 'And maybe I never would have
thought of it, but when I could feel that my son was out
there in the world, oh, I could not endure being away
from him!'

Lakshmi grinned. 'Well, of course. You are Jagadamba.
Your very essence is motherhood, so that makes sense.
Who could be a more ideal mother than you?'

Parvati looked away. 'Sometimes I think I am doing
everything wrong. I went to my father's yajna and ended up
a corpse, separated from Shiva for so many millions of years.
I became a mother without even knowing it and was
separated from my child for years. Shiva and I are

different; time has no meaning for us. Even if millions of years have separated us, we will still be the same when we reunite. But it's different between a mother and child, Lakshmi. The first years of Karthik's life—we will never get that back. Something will always be missing. I do not feel like the ideal mother. And somehow—that *moha* or desire that should never have come has been stirred by his appearance. I want to become a mother again, but properly this time.'

Lakshmi wrapped Parvati into a hug, kissing the top of her hair. 'So be it, sister. Have another child. Why should you not have everything that you want?'

♋

It haunted her for days, this nameless longing for a baby. Parvati became thoughtful and pensive back in Kailash. Shiva grew concerned. It was unlike Parvati to be reticent. He did not want to leave her alone. He followed her around, constantly checking up on her. One day, she was taking a bath. The *ganas* were guarding the door to protect her privacy. She was humming to herself, drying her long, lustrous hair that shone like a mass of black roses over a bed of smoking charcoals scented with *sambhrani*.

She heard Shiva enter the outer chamber, asking for her and demanding to be let in. At first, the *ganas* demurred. She could hear her husband become agitated.

'Uff! Do not get in my way. I need to see my wife.'

The *ganas* feared nothing in this universe other than Shiva. Their resistance collapsed like straws in the wind. Shiva barged into her bathing chamber. 'Parvati! Are you all right?'

Parvati shook her head at him in mock rebuke, touched by his concern for her. 'I am fine! I am just drying my hair.'

'Here, let me help you.' He sat on the stone floor next to her, gathering her hair into his hands. His fingers sifted through her hair, holding the strands tenderly above the fragrant smoke. As her hair dried and he braided it, she leaned against his chest, spreading the towel over herself to keep warm. As he held her in his arm, he used his other hand to massage her scalp. Parvati sighed in bliss.

'What has been on your mind, beloved?'

'I miss Karthik.'

'Miss him? He's right here, next to us.'

'Yes, I know. But I miss the time when he was not ours. When he was truly a child. Now he is always focused on fighting and wars. You won't understand. You bond with him through war and training. He is your son in all ways, but I feel this distance from him that I cannot breach.'

Shiva held her against his chest. Outside it was a moonlit, starry night. Parvati let her eyes drift closed in Shiva's embrace.

'Ask anything of me, Parvati,' he spoke into her hair.

She thought about asking him for another child but was strangely apprehensive. She knew he would do anything for her. But she wanted it to happen naturally through both their desires and not just hers.

೧೦

A few days later, Parvati was again drying herself after a bath. In the distance, she heard Shiva calling for her. *Oh,*

*again the ganas will let him barge in without my permission.
Truly, they are all on his side. The ganas, Nandi, even Karthik.
There should be one who cares for me, who is with me always.*

Just then, a few beads of her sweat hit the floor and
transformed into a radiant, handsome boy. He was dusky
rose in complexion and had a small round belly—the
sweetest child she had ever seen. He was short but had
large inquisitive eyes that gleamed with curiosity and
intellect. His elbows and legs were chubby and dimpled.
He was swaddled in a tiny yellow dhoti.

A rush of maternal love came over Parvati. *My son!
Born in such a miraculous way!* She wanted to immediately
hold him and coo over him, but she needed to get
properly dressed first. She needed to tell Shiva, too. She
pointed at the door.

'Go guard the door, my child. And be sure not to
allow anyone in.'

He dutifully padded to the door, opened it and closed
it behind him.

Parvati was giddy with delight as she wore her
brightest red sari and painted kohl over her eyes. She had
never known such happiness before. And how charmed
Shiva would be by this sweet child! She memorised the
features of his face. How handsome he was, how deva-
like. He reminded her of Karthik, too, and she could not
wait for both of them to meet. Karthik would watch over
him as his elder brother. This would keep him close to
home, too, giving him something to do other than fight
wars. They would be a complete family.

In the meantime, a band of *ganas* had come to let
Parvati know that Shiva was looking for her. The boy
directed them to stand back. He walked a distance away

from the chamber to meet them. He did not want to disturb her bath with the sound of their voices.

The *ganas* dealt with him patiently. 'Come on, get out of the way. Our master, Shiva, wants to see his wife.'

He cocked his head to the side innocently. 'I have been ordered not to let anybody in at all.'

The *ganas* looked at each other. 'Who is this fellow?' One of them asked. 'We have never seen him before. Is he an asura come to fight our master and mistress?' The *ganas* were now agitated and heckled the boy.

They surrounded the boy and started poking him. 'Who are you? What is your name? Where did you come from?'

He cocked his head to the side again. 'I do not know,' he answered truthfully.

The *ganas* became outraged. They started beating him.

From a distance, Shiva and Nandi noticed the commotion. Shiva asked, 'What is going on? Come on, Nandi. We had better investigate.'

By the time Shiva and Nandi reached them, the boy had already beaten back and destroyed all the *ganas* who had opposed him. They rolled on the ground, some unconscious and some groaning in pain. The boy was untouched and smiling serenely. He nodded politely and formally as Shiva and Nandi approached him.

Shiva was alarmed to see hundreds of his *ganas* incapacitated. He grabbed the boy and held him by the throat.

His voice was icy steel as he asked, 'Who are you? What is the meaning of this? Why have you come here?'

Before the boy could answer, Shiva yelled loudly, 'Parvati! Are you safe?'

'Yes! I'm just coming out, Shiva. Give me a few minutes.'

'No! Stay inside. I will tell you when it is safe to come out.' He did not want her to get involved in this trouble.

His hand tightened around the boy's neck. What kind of supernatural power did he possess if he was able to single-handedly defeat the *ganas*? Was he a new asura here to torment and attack the devas? The boy pointed at his hand to indicate that he was unable to talk while Shiva was choking him.

Shiva relaxed his grip, slightly. 'Who are you and what are you doing here?' He demanded again.

'I am guarding her door. I am under strict instructions not to let anybody enter.' His voice was tremulous, but his recent antics proved he was not to be underestimated.

No one dared interfere with Shiva and his wife. The hair at the back of Shiva's neck stood up. For a moment, he remembered Daksha and his yajna, the last time he had been separated from her. *I would never let that happen again. Nobody would ever keep me away from her.*

All the devas carried with them weapons of some sort. But Shiva had all weapons at his command within him. In less time than it took the boy to blink his large, limpid eyes, the sword appeared in Shiva's hand and he sliced off the boy's head.

As the corpse fell from his hands, Parvati called out, 'Can I come out now?'

'Yes,' he replied absent-mindedly. He stared at the corpse and felt a pang of regret. There was something about the boy that seemed familiar. A yawning gap opened up inside him, a bottomless pit of loss.

Before he could tell Parvati to wait a bit longer, she came out in her finest red sari. Her hair was tied up elaborately. She rarely adorned herself, but today she wore golden bracelets and necklaces, her lips tinted crimson, eyes lined in kohl. Even around her red bindi, she had painted a design with vermilion and sandalwood paste. Shiva had never seen her look so beautiful. Her face was wreathed with a smile of such joy and love that his heart stammered.

He looked away before she could see what he had done.

♋

The world could perhaps withstand the fury of Shiva. But it could not brave the fury of Shakti. Parvati's ferocious wail roused all the *ganas*, who clapped their hands around their ears to block out that desolate sound. Her eyes struck like lightning those who dared to meet her fierce gaze. Most simply collapsed on the ground before her. She unfurled her form as Durga, her eight arms wielding a mace, sword, disc, arrow and trident. The weapons began whirling above her hands, whipping winds so strong that they levelled faraway mountains, reaching out beyond Kailash to the mortal worlds, raising tsunamis out of seas, sandstorms in unexplored deserts. With each expulsion of breath, volcanoes erupted and earthquakes shattered continents. The thrones of Indra and the other devas shook with the force of her wrath.

Innumerable yoginis manifested around her. At her behest, they were ready to create a great deluge that would swallow up the worlds and destroy even the devas.

Shiva was already remorseful about the death of the boy. Now he fell before her, head low, desperate to pacify her.

'Parvati, I am sorry.'

She hissed, 'My son has been killed! I will not let this pass.'

Shiva looked up, face blank from shock. 'Your son? We have another one?'

The devas had by now thronged to Kailash. They massed at her feet and prostrated themselves before her, begging for her to show mercy.

'So long as my son is dead, I shall not be at peace.'

Shiva stepped before her. 'It was I who killed him, Devi. I will fix this.'

'It cannot be fixed. You cannot bring back to life what is already dead.' She began trembling with rage.

'He just needs a new head. Just wait and see, Devi.'

She relented with a regal nod of her head.

Shiva whistled to summon the *ganas*. They were beside themselves as they realised the tragedy that had taken place. Their faces were snotty with tears, hair rumpled and sticking up in different directions from pulling at it.

Shiva commanded them, 'Listen to me! We have no time to lose. All of you go in the northern direction. Bring for me the first head that you see. With that, I will resuscitate my son.'

The *ganas* left immediately, accompanied by the devas and other celestials. They were all desperate to quell the grief of Parvati, to restore harmony and balance to the cosmos once more. Within minutes, they came back to Shiva with the first head they had found.

Shiva glanced at the one-tusked elephant head they had brought back. He lifted a quizzical brow.

Nandi answered helpfully, 'It was the first being with a head that we encountered—a one-tusked elephant. So, we brought the head back for you.'

Shiva sighed. Sometimes the *ganas* were a bit too literal. But they had followed his word and his word could not be broken. He carefully washed and sanctified the head and the boy's body. He joined the two together with auspicious chants and the force of his meditation.

Thus was born Ganesha, the second son of Shiva and Parvati. Shiva was so impressed by the boy's valour against the *ganas* and his steadfast loyalty to his mother that he immediately appointed him the new chief of the *ganas*.

Shiva gently carried him in his arms to Parvati. He did not want her to be shocked, so he asked her to close her eyes. When she opened her eyes, she could not stifle her gasp of horror. For a moment, a shadow passed over Ganesha's eyes. Parvati was brought back to the moment of her *vahana* ceremony when she had assumed the form of Kali. She remembered the look of disgust on her father, how it had made her shrink into herself.

This was her son. It was Shiva who had taught her to see beauty at a deeper level, in a different way. In the second blink of her eyes, she saw how adorable her son was, the wisdom that shone from his elephantine head. For the first time, she understood how Shiva delighted in her manifold forms, some of which were fierce and terrifying and some gentle and girlish. She felt the same for her son, a love that went beyond name and form. She stretched out her arms to embrace him.

Ganesha was undoubtedly unique, with his squat form, large potbelly and the head of a one-tusked elephant. Yet he endeared himself to everyone; they even found his appearance lovable. The devas bowed before him. Relieved that he had been saved, they appointed Ganesha the first among the devas to be worshipped, the one who removed all obstacles.

He was a veritable treasure trove of wisdom yet was also content to be a baby who cuddled with his parents as they fed him *modakas*, his favourite sweet. He played and frolicked all across Kailash with his pet mouse, Mushika. There were those who were partial to Narayana or Shiva or Parvati or Karthik, but everyone loved Ganesha. He was able to quickly resolve disputes and solve riddles, politely and with a smile.

The only one he did not always get along with was his brother, Karthik.

CHAPTER 19

All siblings have rivalry. But a rivalry between two brothers who also happen to be extraordinarily powerful devas could be quite a dangerous thing, as Shiva and Parvati soon found out.

The time had come for Ganesha and Karthik to get married.

Shiva and Parvati loved playing games and delighted each other with challenges and riddles all the time. They debated and discussed arcane topics of meditation and yoga into the late hours, in faraway caves and on the banks of Himalayan lakes. The words of their conversations became sacred texts that continued to inspire and teach mortals for millions of years.

They turned their sons' nuptials into a game too. They declared that the brother who raced around the world the fastest would be the first to marry. Both their sons were beloved to them. Rather than choose whom to marry off first, they thought an objective contest would be the fair way to decide. They thought this was harmless, for their games had only sweetened their love for each other.

So, with great fanfare, the competition was announced. When the boys heard the news, Ganesha looked down at his round belly and short legs. He exhaled in dismay. Karthik grinned, his almond-shaped hazel eyes gleaming triumphantly. The rivalry between the brothers had become legendary. This, however, was the first time that their parents were allowing them to compete openly.

All the devas and *gandharvas* flocked to Kailash, eager to watch the race. They placed bets, almost all of them putting their odds on Karthik. He was the commander of the armies of the devas, a seasoned warrior who could battle the asuras for years on end without breaking for food or sleep. And Ganesha—well, he mostly enjoyed eating sweet *modakas* and following Parvati everywhere, his gait ponderous as he mused on the various riddles of the universe. He had become extremely dear to Lakshmi, who pampered him with more *modakas* than even he could consume.

The more discriminating of the devas and *gandharvas* knew better than to count Ganesha out. He had wisdom on his side. While Shiva delighted in bestowing upon Karthik various divine weapons, he enjoyed posing intricate questions to Ganesha about yoga, spiritual alchemy and the esoteric doctrines of tantra. Ganesha tested out different theories with his mother until he could formulate a response. When his answers pleased Shiva (as they always did), he was rewarded with a smile as bright as the moon. While his body could sometimes be slow, his quicksilver mind was unparalleled.

Thus, while some *gandharvas* clucked sympathetically over Ganesha's probable loss, others simply held their tongue and waited to see what would happen.

No one was more excited for the race than the mischief-maker, Narada. He was practically clapping in eagerness for the event to start.

Narayana stood next to him and crossed his arms over his sapphire blue chest. 'It is a bad sign if you are so happy about this competition, Narada. It means there is going to be trouble for us, does it not?'

Narada snorted. 'You hardly need me to tell you that. I realise parenting is not a common pastime in Devaloka, but surely Shiva and Parvati know better than to pit these two against each other. It could turn violent.'

'We all see the world as we see ourselves. Shiva and Parvati have never experienced rivalry or jealousy, so they cannot conceive of it existing in their sons. They think of such contests as innocuous fun, like their own mock love quarrels.'

'Shouldn't you try to talk them out of this?'

It was Narayana's turn to snort. 'It is never advisable to interfere in another family's affairs, Devarishi. And nowadays it is impossible to get a hold of these two. Either they are secluded by themselves or they are busy with their children or they are off dealing with all the mortals who pray to them so devoutly.'

Narada sighed. 'I have a bad feeling about this one.'

Narayana turned to him. 'Whatever happens, do not meddle and make it worse, Narada.'

Narada shrugged sheepishly. That he could not promise. Being a troublemaker was part of his nature, something he could not control. But he served a larger purpose, too. He was not just a nuisance. Sometimes the world of the devas needed to be shaken out of complacency. Sometimes they needed a bit of trouble. And this was going to be trouble.

A thousand conches were sounded to officially start the race. Instantly, Karthik took off on Paravani, his peacock *vahana*. The peacock suited him. He was beautiful, lithe, elegant. He smoothly spread his blue-green wings and lifted off with Karthik on his slender back.

Ganesha's *vahana* was Mushika, the mouse. They all had been bemused by the choice of a mouse for the large, hulking Ganesha. But it ended up suiting him perfectly, too.

Mushika scampered to Ganesha. He may have been tiny, but he was determined to do his level best to help Ganesha win. Ganesha looked at him with a benevolent smile and fondly patted him on the head.

Mushika shifted from one foot to another anxiously. He squeaked, 'Shouldn't we go? There is much ground to cover. We have to cross seven continents and many seas. Your brother has already left. We have to at least try to catch up!'

The *gandharvas* and devas watched from clouds high above Kailash. They were aghast that Ganesha was simply sitting in place while his brother had zoomed out of sight in a whirlwind of dust. *Had he given up already?* They tut-tutted.

Ganesha's trunk moved rhythmically from one side to another as he deliberated over the situation. 'It is no use, Mushika. There is no way I can defeat my brother in a physical contest. We will have to find another way.'

How can I go around the world quickly?

Ganesha looked towards his parents. They were looking at him, perturbed. He waved at them cheerfully so that they would not worry. Normally, if he were stuck or had a question, he would go to them for guidance. But it would be unfair to do so in the current situation. His trunk thumped in sudden inspiration. He had an idea.

Ganesha got on his feet and walked away. He went to his house and entered the bathing chambers. He washed himself and returned holding two *kusha* grass mats. He asked Mushika to clear some space on the ground and cleaned it thoroughly. After it was made immaculate, Ganesha carefully spread the two mats and approached his parents. He asked them to be seated on the mats. They looked at each other in confusion but complied.

Once they had been seated, Ganesha bowed to them reverentially and slowly walked around them seven times. After he completed the seventh circumambulation, he rubbed his hands together gleefully.

'There! I have finished circling the world and have won the race!'

The surrounding devas and *gandharvas* cried out in bewilderment. Ganesha never told a lie. Yet, how could he have won the race?

Ganesha explained, 'For me, my parents are the source of everything. They are my world. By circumambulating them, I have indeed gone around the world seven times. What need have I for anything else in this world when they are with me?' There was no sophistry in his voice, only sincerity.

With anyone else, it may not have worked. Narayana would have insisted on being more meticulous about the rules. Yama would have rolled his eyes at the metaphor, strict as he was about justice and weighing one's good and bad actions. But Shiva and Parvati were delighted. They relished this kind of play on words, the riddles with which they expressed their love for each other. Before their other son returned, they proclaimed Ganesha the winner. And because Shiva's word was so potent, immediately the wedding preparations commenced.

In the meantime, Karthik raced madly through deserts, foaming oceans, narrow passes at such high speed that the mountains trembled in his wake. He did not bother to see if his younger brother was behind him. Ever the consummate warrior, he had a single-minded focus on the destination. No one could defeat him so long as he controlled himself, allowing no distraction.

He enjoyed flying. He had always liked travelling, had come into the world with a restless spirit full of wanderlust. His parents and brother were content to isolate themselves away in Kailash, but he never felt he truly belonged there. He often thought of his six foster mothers wistfully—their earthy banter and easy laughter as they washed themselves and their clothes in the river. He had never visited them after he had come to Kailash, knowing he would only sharpen their heartbreak. But it took a toll on him keeping his distance from them.

The journey invigorated him. As they landed in a cloud of dust on Kailash, Karthik was cheerful. Perhaps he would take Ganesha for a ride later. Paravani was sturdy enough for both of them. *That little mouse was useless*, Karthik thought. Sometimes his brother was just strange.

Perhaps things would have been different if Narada had not been the first one to greet him. But Narada had his designs, too. As Karthik fetched a bucket of water to wash his face, hands and feet before presenting himself to his parents, Narada rushed to his side.

Karthik eyed him suspiciously. Shiva had warned him to be wary of the mischievous sage.

'What is it, Devarishi?' He asked in a clipped tone, splashing glacial water onto his fair cheeks.

Narada wrung his hands. 'Oh, my dear boy, I just wanted to prepare you for the shock of it, to at least spare you the humiliation of discovering what happened in public.'

Karthik rolled his eyes. 'Always so much drama, Devarishi.' He was quite sanguine that he had won the race. How could that waddling elephant-headed brother of his have kept up with him? And even if he had lost, Karthik was not so arrogant that he would begrudge his brother a fairly earned victory.

'But it was not fair.'

Karthik's back stiffened. It irritated him how this peculiar sage could so easily read his mind. He began striding towards the wooden platform where his parents were waiting. The platform had been hurriedly constructed for the contest, to accommodate the swarms of curious onlookers. Kailash had never been so crowded. Karthik's refined sense of hearing, honed over countless years of intense warfare, picked up the excited chatter from the crowd. He also heard the drone of brahmanas chanting the Vedas, as if they were officiating a ceremony.

At Karthik's frown, Narada clucked sympathetically. 'I did not believe it either. But they have already married him off, my child.'

Karthik accelerated his pace. 'They would not do that to me.' Anger and disbelief crept from his gut to his forehead. When he reached the platform, he saw that Narada was correct. Ganesha was being married off—to two beautiful girls! He was practically hopping in happiness. They had not even waited for him to attend his brother's wedding. Karthik stormed away on the back of Paravani. His anger was so palpable that the ground of Kailash shook. But he was long gone before anybody could notice.

♋

Karthik had come to Krauncha Mountain. He sat facing south, away from Kailash.

It was Shiva who came after him. He was the one closest to Karthik. Shiva dismounted from Nandi's back and walked hesitantly towards his son. He stood behind him, weighing his words. He had mastered all sixty-four arts and forms of knowledge, but he did not know how to do this. Emotions, the messiness of family relations, all of that was beyond his ken.

Karthik said sullenly, 'How did you find me?'

Shiva smothered a smile. As hardened a warrior and wise beyond his years as his son was, he could still behave like any pouting teenage boy.

'There is nowhere you could go in this universe where I would not find you, son.'

Karthik harrumphed. 'You did not even know of my existence the first years of my life.'

Karthik was balanced on a rock, practising his military exercises. He stood gracefully on a single toe, eyes closed, hovering over the precipice. Shiva joined his son on the rock. For a few moments, Shiva gazed at the landscape spread beneath their feet. It was quite a bit south of the Himalayas, where his usual haunts were. It was hotter here, and the mountains were shorter, covered in scrub rather than tall pine forests. Instead of snow, grasslands and rolling pastures surrounded them.

Shiva remarked, 'It's quite beautiful here. I do not think I have been here before.'

Karthik reluctantly sat down next to his father. 'That was the point, you know. You wouldn't like a place like this. From here, you can see the common people and lands lived upon by the mortals. It is not hidden like Kailash.'

'Hmm.'

'I am not coming back.' Karthik's voice was calm yet firm.

Shiva sighed. 'We did not handle it well, my boy. I grant you that. We are the first of the devas to be parents and our family is unique, to say the least.'

'It has nothing to do with being a parent. It is a simple matter of right and wrong. That boy won through a deceptive trick and you let him get away with it. You preside over the worlds and know better than that. Your softness for him coloured your judgment. It is as simple as that.'

Shiva was at a loss. Not the type to feel emotions himself, he did not feel equipped to deal with all the layers of feeling in his son's pained, bitter voice. 'It is not so simple, Karthik.'

Karthik snorted. 'Of course, it is. In your heart, you know that it was wrong. That is why you rushed to have the ceremony over with as soon as possible, to avoid objection and your own guilt.'

Shiva leapt to his feet and began pacing the narrow mountainside path from where the stone upon which they sat jutted out. 'The truth is, Karthik, we rushed because once the race was over, we were worried about how you would react. Also, once my word has been given, it must come to fruition immediately. In any event, we thought it would be easier if we finished before you were back.'

'You underestimated my speed.'

Shiva inclined his head. 'That is true. You were unbelievably fast, son. I'm very proud of you.'

'Not fast enough to beat that fraud.'

'That fraud is your brother. It was not a trick. It was another interpretation of the rules of the contest. And it was an intelligent and creative one. As a military strategist, you must appreciate this. I do wish the two of you would get along better. There is much you could learn from each other.'

Karthik tightened his jaw. 'Why do you say that to only me? You never say anything to him. All your lectures are for me, never him. I guess you still feel guilty after beheading him all those years ago.'

Shiva chuckled. 'It was not one of my finer moments,' he acknowledged.

'I guess I get my hot temper from you.' Karthik could not suppress a small smile.

Shiva patted him on the back affectionately. 'The temper is okay. The world needs our anger sometimes, too. But do not be so stubborn. I was like that, too, once. I thought I was meant to be eternally alone in isolation. Then your mother came along, and I realised there were parts of me I did not know existed. She made me grow and evolve, become all that I can be. That is what a family does, son. And we are family. You need us and we need you. Do not turn your back on us.'

'Don't you think it would have been much better if we had never been born, though? You would have been free of all this mess and drama.'

'Better? No. Easier, perhaps. But not better.'

Karthik did not respond. His eyes were fixed on a distant point in the horizon. His eyes were the softest part of him. The rest of his body was that of a hardened warrior, but his eyes were those of a poet.

Shiva said gently, 'We have been searching all the worlds for the best wife or wives for you, son. We have some suitable candidates...'

Karthik shook his head adamantly. 'No. I will never marry somebody you choose for me.'

Shiva swallowed. Karthik was too polite to say it, so Shiva said it for him.

'Do you want me to leave, Karthik? Is that what you want? To live as if we do not even exist? Is that how much anger there is in you?'

Karthik nodded curtly.

Resigned, Shiva said, 'So be it,' and left.

♋

Parvati was distraught. She made Shiva replay his conversation with Karthik over and over again, verbatim. Every time she tried to visit Karthik, he turned her away. Even Ganesha could not comfort her.

No one in Kailash or Mount Meru was able to help her. The devas and *gandharvas* lacked children for the most part and had no practical advice to offer. Many of the rishis were married, but their familial lives seemed as idyllic as their ashrams.

One evening, as Shiva inhaled a puff of chillum, he remarked, 'You may as well go to the human worlds. It seems they are the only other ones who have this kind of trouble. Maybe they can help.'

Parvati sighed. 'They are the ones who pray to us to get a happy marriage and family life. What would they think if they knew about all of this?'

Shiva drew her into his embrace. 'I think they would understand more than we expect.'

ॐ

Shiva woke Parvati excitedly in the middle of the night. 'I have figured it out, Devi.'

Parvati rubbed her eyes sleepily. 'What is wrong, Shiva?' She reached for his arms, strong as trees, to reassure herself he was still there. Sometimes she still had nightmares that they had been separated again.

Shiva tightened his embrace. 'I have an idea of how we can bring our family together again.'

'How?' She sat up, fully alert now. Her pale face turned towards Shiva like a flower that bloomed under the light of the moon.

'Well, I was thinking that the devas are also like a family. We often bicker and have rivalries amongst ourselves. But there is always one thing that brings us together without fail. Do you know what that is?'

Parvati shook her head with a smile of anticipation.

'A common enemy! For us, that's always been the asuras. We need a common enemy that our family must unite to defeat.'

'Do we have one?' Her voice quivered dubiously.

'Oh yes, there's a giant enemy out there perfect for this. I've been trying to figure out what to do about this one. Now I realise we are the ones who must fight him. The only way he can die is at our hands. Only the four of us together can defeat him. Devi, together, the four of us shall destroy Tripura.'

CHAPTER 20

Sometimes the devas were too kind for their own good. Especially when they were asked for boons. They never could say no to someone on their knees who had done the requisite *tapas* and sincerely asked for a favour. Usually, it was immortality. But immortality could not be granted by the devas. Loathe to send a devotee away unsatisfied, they came up with compromises that offered the prospect of immortality without guaranteeing it with some difficult loopholes.

And so it was that the three sons of Tarakasura—the asura who had been defeated by Karthik—had become immensely powerful through the boon they had sought from Brahma. They wanted immortality and Brahma said it was impossible. Then they asked for impregnable fortresses that would last forever; Brahma said nothing could be everlasting. They included a caveat in the request—the destruction of the cities they would inhabit could only be brought about by the shooting of a single arrow. That appeased Brahma and they got their boon.

The lowest city, built of iron, was located on Earth. The middle city, built of silver, was placed in the sky.

And the topmost city, with walls of gold, was built in Swarga. Only for a few moments every thousand years or so, when the Pushya constellation was in conjunction with the moon, would the cities be aligned. Only at that moment was their destruction possible.

Asuras began flocking to Tripura now that they had this marvellous safe haven. At first, the devas were worried about the increasing power of the asuras. They came to Shiva for help in defeating the asuras. He shrugged them off. He would not attack anyone who was not directly causing harm. It was when the asuras began openly fighting the devas and attacking innocent mortals that Shiva agreed to act.

The whole host of celestials had approached him in Kailash. It was a beautiful sight, thousands of devas and rishis arrayed before him, fanning out against the backdrop of snowy mountain peaks. Their elegant pale robes fluttered in the cold wind. They waited in hushed silence for his pronouncement.

Shiva was never one for formality. He did not explain. He simply announced, 'This is one battle we must fight together. Not just me but my entire family and all of you.'

Shiva coaxed his family to come together for the fight. Ganesha appeared instantly. Karthik had to be summoned, but he could not resist a dharmic war and came quickly, too. In the time he had been away, Karthik had obtained two wives of his own and had grown into his full splendour as a deva.

Parvati generated manifestations of fierce yoginis, who massed into armies and fought alongside the devas. Karthik assumed his characteristic position as the commander of the devas. For a long time, the devas fought valorously against the asuras. But the city of Tripura had within it a pool that revived those who had fallen in the war. The asuras kept coming back to life, fully invigorated, even as the devas grew fatigued. It was a never-ending battle.

At the desperate moment, as they always did, the devas turned to Shiva. He told them what was to be done. In preparation for the impending moment when the three cities of Tripura would be aligned, a chariot the likes of which had never been seen was constructed under his instruction. Earth itself became the chariot. The sun and moon were its wheels. Brahma held the reins. Mount Meru became the bow and Vasuki the serpent became the bowstring. Narayana was the arrow. Agni was the tip of the arrow. Vayu, the god of the winds, was inside the feathers on the rear of the arrow to give it more velocity. Each deva had their place in the chariot.

The cities of Tripura were about to align. Shiva, along with the devas and warriors, including Karthik, bowed down to Ganesha, the one to whom all worship was offered before any propitious moment. Then, Shiva strung and raised the mighty bow in a fluid movement. The twang of the arrow was enough to make the multiverse tremble.

At the last moment, Shiva did not release the arrow. He simply smiled. The three cities of Tripura were instantly incinerated. At first, the devas were awed, but then, as they realised Shiva had been capable of this all along and never needed the chariot or them, their spirits deflated. Shiva, in his compassion, fired the arrow on the cities even as they were burning to honour the efforts of all the devas and warriors.

Later, as the devas began dispersing to their homes, Narayana asked Shiva why he had done that. 'Why did you gather all the armies, let them expend so much energy and time in fruitless battles, instructed them to construct such an elaborate chariot, when none of it was needed. Was it to make a mockery out of them?'

Shiva shook his head. 'My friend, I did not even plan to do it that way. I thought I would shoot the arrow. But I realised something at that moment that made me smile. And just like that, without even thinking it, the adharmic Tripura was destroyed immediately.'

Narayana turned to him curiously. 'And what was it you realised?'

Shiva's head turned away from Narayana. He watched as Karthik and Ganesha good-naturedly ribbed each other, play-wrestling and teasing, the way brothers should. He watched as Parvati shook her head and smiled at their antics. His breath bated as it always did when her eyes lifted and met his, when her smile transformed into something else that belonged to them and them alone.

'I realised I could have done it on my own. You could have done it alone, too. And so could my wife. After all, we are omniscient, omnipotent and omnipresent. But there is sweeter pleasure in doing it together, as a family and as a pantheon.'

Narayana hid his smile. He had never thought he would hear such words from Shiva. But one thing *kaala*, Time, had taught him was that all things, even devas, could change. Sometimes they just needed a push. Or a little love.

CHAPTER 21

'Idid not know there was such a thing as a family portrait for devas,' remarked Parvati wryly.

Shiva grinned. 'That is because we are the first family among the devas.'

It was not a portrait, not exactly. Such things did not exist then. It was a time when mortals still beheld the immortals and did not need engraved images for what could be seen by their eyes. But the rishis wanted to capture the image in their mind's eye to transmit for generations and millennia to come.

Shiva sat next to Parvati, and they were flanked by both of their sons. Karthik still lived south of the Krauncha Mountain. But they had hammered out an arrangement whereby for ten days in a year, the entire family would congregate. During this time Parvati would come down to the mortal world and reunite with her family. The rest of the time, they led their own lives, or Shiva and Parvati roamed on their own. It was not conventional, perhaps, but it worked for them.

Parvati chuckled. 'What an odd assortment we make.' With gold bangles dancing on her delicate wrists, she indicated their family. Shiva, Parvati, Ganesha, Karthik and, next to them, their *vahanas*—Nandi, the bull, for Shiva, who also wore a snake; Dawon, the lion, for Parvati; Mushika, the mouse, for Ganesha; and Paravani, the peacock, for Karthik. She still marvelled at how this family of hers had come together. Not even the rishis or devas could have predicted this. She could never have dreamt it in all those journeys she made to the moons, in all her daydreaming hours as a girl on Mount Meru.

Shiva raised a finger. 'My beloved wife, you must look at it differently. In the real world, the lion considers the bull to be prey and the bull fears the lion. The snake hunts the mouse, and the peacock hunts the snake. Here, though, out of love, even those who are natural enemies become friendly toward each other and become family. However much we may clash or differ, we still come together as a family and coexist in harmony. There is much profound truth to be learned through this.'

Parvati wore a sly smile on her face.

Mid-lecture, Shiva stopped and narrowed his eyes at her suspiciously. 'Were you deliberately provoking me into saying that?'

A peal of laughter escaped from her lips as she nodded in confession. 'It is not the first time I have played a trick on you, husband.'

Shiva tenderly brushed a strand of hair behind her ear and pressed her earlobe affectionately.

'And it will not be the last,' he promised.

EPILOGUE / PROLOGUE

Emerging from the misty fog of time, Ardhanarishvara stepped forth. This was the most complete deity in the universe, Shiva and Shakti melded into one. The left side was Parvati, fair and dressed in pink, adorned with flowers and gems. The right side was Shiva, dressed in tiger skin, blue-grey, adorned by a snake, his hand holding aloft a trident. In this composite form, the male and female principles became inseparable. The passive force of the universe and the feminine active force, always drawn to each other to embrace and fuse with each other, to bring out the best in each other. They were a One that was beyond any concept of Two—uniting within themself the material world and the spiritual, the path of the ascetic and the path of the householder, the qualities of the feminine and those of the masculine, eternally braided together.

Ardhanarishvara sighed. It was time again to play the game. They separated into two reluctantly.

Shiva took Shakti's hand. 'Devi, it is time. Shall we start this once again?'

She nodded. They smiled, knowing any separation would only be temporary. There would be variation, there would be differences. But always, always, they would come back to each other. To this, to a union that was greater than the sum of their selves.

They leapt. It was time to play again.

ABOUT THE AUTHOR

 Aditi Banerjee is the author of *The Curse of Gandhari* and a practicing attorney at a Fortune 500 financial services company. She recently earned an executive MBA from Columbia University. She has published several essays on Hinduism and the Hindu-American experience in publications such as *The Columbia Documentary History of Religion in America since 1945* and *Buddhists, Hindus, and Sikhs in America*. In her free time, she enjoys wandering the Himalayas and experimenting with new recipes in the kitchen.